# Recovering

## A Gabe Fox Novella

Girl with Broken Wings, 3.5

J Bennett

ISBN: 978-0-9910566-9-9

This is a work of fiction. Names, characters, places and incidents either are the product of the author's imagination or are used fictitiously, and any resemblance to actual persons, living or dead, business establishments, events or locales is entirely coincidental.

The publisher does not have any control over and does not assume any responsibility for third-party websites or their content

# A Note To The Reader

Dear Reader,

Thank you so much for your interest in RECOVERING, a novella written from the point of view of Gabe Fox. After I completed RISING, book three in the GIRL WITH BROKEN WINGS series, I realized something was missing.

Not enough Gabe (or cowbell).

Gabe's personality was just too big, too important to be silenced for so long. As I wrote RISING, a second story started forming in the back of my mind. Gabe's story. This story. RECOVERING takes place after LANDING, book two in the GIRL WITH BROKEN WINGS series, and the events in the novella run parallel to the first half of RISING.

While you *can* read this novella directly after LANDING, I strongly suggest that you read RISING first to get a greater sense of the events that motivated Gabe to act. If this is your first selection in the GIRL WITH BROKEN WINGS series, I encourage you to start from the beginning with FALLING before reading this. Gabe's situation and mindset are directly related to events that have occurred in the previous books in the series.

One last little note. Gabe is a passionate person. He likes to cuss, and he likes to tell you exactly what he thinks about...pretty much everything. The previous books in this series have included strong language, but Gabe's novella pushes the line a little further. I considered cleaning him up...but I couldn't. Gabe is Gabe, and that's exactly why I love him. I hope you do too!

Enjoy,

J Bennett

# *Chapter 1*

One pushup. Just one fucking pushup.

I get down into position. Even this is hard. Everything is hard now. Every last thing. I plant my hands wide, center my body between my palms and toes and lower myself down.

Sweat beads across my brow. Keira Knightley gives me a broody stare. My muscles tremble, and I pant like a dog in heat.

There was a time not too long ago when I could do fifty pushups without stopping. Easy peasy. When I could deadlift 350 and spar with Tarren for an hour without breaking a sweat. Okay, maybe a little sweat, but I could duck and dodge like Quicksilver and even take Tarren's hits when I had to.

And now? A gust of wind could blow me over.

My elbows bend to 90 degrees, and my stomach brushes the floor. Halfway there. Now I just have to push up. How hard can it be? I only just broke 100 pounds on the scale last week.

I try. I really fucking try. I push and use all the good curses I know. Then the not so good ones. I even cuss out farm animals though I gave that trick away to Maya. But I'm not going anywhere. My arms collapse, and I'm a puddle of pathetic, wheezing on the floor of the basement, trying to stop my vision from spinning. Aches wake up in just about every joint in my body.

And Kiera's still watching. Judging.

Her sultry eyes bring me to my knees. I can't stand that stare, the complete disaster she's looking at. I turn the cardboard figure to the wall. The anger bubbles up, and I kick the big rubber ball we keep down here with the other exercise equipment, sending it skidding into the wall.

Strip clubs. Maya and Tarren are actually going undercover in skank-tastic strip clubs right now! How many times have I gotten on my knees and prayed to God for a mission that actually legit required us to visit dozens of strip clubs and perhaps rescue some extra jiggly damsels in distress? Okay, maybe not on my knees, but that prayer was always in my heart. And here it is, titties served up on a platter, and Tarren's the one getting all the exposure. And the big dolt won't enjoy a second of it. I guarantee you.

I drag my ass to the brown, patched couch we have down here and sink into its lumpy cushions. Tammy fell in love with this dumpster treasure the moment she saw it hanging on some curb in La Junta. When Mom refused to pick it up, Tammy dragged me out with her that night to load it in my truck and sneak it in the house. An hour's drive each way for a couch so ugly the *Pawn Star* guys would probably pay me a $1,000 to keep it. That was Tammy, all heart and stubbornness and a dash of crazy.

I lean back on the couch and do that thing I really, really hate doing.

I think about what happened.

Drained. In a single word, that's the gist of it. Touched by an angel in a very bad way.

My energy was literally pulled out of my body by a sicko fuck named Grand. Five years ago that bastard killed Tammy. Maya and Tarren won't tell me shit about what happened when he drained me three months ago back in October, but I know it was close.

My memory of that month is Swiss cheese. Ghostly images flicker in my mind – a big circus tent, a breath mint tangled in my hair, mopping a floor – but they tell only pieces of a story that leads to a big, black empty hole. Somewhere in that hole Grand kidnapped Tarren. Maya and I went after him. He drained me. He died.

I wish I could remember. I wish I could have looked into Grand's eyes and watched the light fade. Maybe it would help me be at peace with Tammy. Probably not, though.

Dr. Lee says this whole memory gap thing is normal with traumatic incidents. Something about how memories take time to settle and become permanent. If something interrupts that process, like, say, a skull fracture and then a five-day coma on top of it, the memories just evaporate.

Poof. Gone. Just me waking up with a feeding tube down my throat and a horrifying skeletal body tucked under the covers. Apparently my body tried to compensate for the energy drain by feeding on itself like it was Shark Week. It's not like I was all muscular and brawny like Tarren in the first place. He can swing a 5-pound kettlebell once and come away with bulging biceps and a six pack. Me, I had to work for what little I had, and now...yeah, now even a cardboard cutout is laughing at me.

Even though Maya and Tarren won't tell me what happened the night I got drained, I have a pretty good idea of what went down. I see the way Maya looks at me. The guilt. I must have screwed up. Big time. Grand took Tarren, and I probably went bat shit all over the place. I can see myself storming in, guns blazing, and getting drained on the spot. Maya saved me. Saved Tarren. Still won't tell me how she went all Wonder Woman and killed the most powerful, most evil, biggest boss villain in the world. If I flamed out the way I suspect, she probably thinks she's doing me the mother of all favors by not pulling the curtain up on my epic fail.

Okay, this pity party is officially over. I'm taking the stairs by storm.

By storm, I mean one at a time. Each foot comes down with purpose and up I go. I don't stop until I reach the top and then I pause for a couple of seconds to breathe.

"Tomorrow," I say to myself. "Tomorrow I will do a pushup."

Tomorrow Keira will be proud of me. Until then, I need to chill.

The house is too big, too empty without Tarren and Maya. Filled with too many ghosts. Every slow second is a reminder that I've been left behind. Too much of a burden to go on the mission, though I was the one who discovered the trail of dead strippers, like hot, murdered breadcrumbs scattered across the country. Lot of thanks I got for it too. Just Maya's constant harping over calories and hydration. She means well. I know this, but it would almost be better if she completely ignored me like Tarren does. I'd rather be treated like a leper than like a 5-year-old with a high temperature.

I hear a knock on the front door, and for a full two seconds I fritz out like a 1990's PC trying to load the latest WOW expansion pack. No one comes to our house. Ever. Not even the mail guy. I have everything routed to a P.O. box.

*Angels.*

After that epic pause I scramble for a gun. Mom taught us to stay armed at all times, even in the house, especially in the house. If they ever found us, the attack would come quickly, and we'd need to react immediately. When Tarren is here, I'm usually good about Mom's rules, which are now his rules.

But Tarren hasn't been around, and the only thing I'm currently packing is crumbs from the Doritos I had for breakfast. Or was that lunch? I know I had one of my Beretta PX4s in the waistband of my jeans at one point, but that was, how long ago? Hell, I don't even know what day it is. They all run together like someone put on a record called "Gabe does nothing while Maya and Tarren go to strip clubs" and left it on constant repeat.

I spin around in a little circle in the kitchen hoping to spot a gun on the counter or the table. Whew, I think every single plate and cup we own is fermenting in the sink. Should probably clean those if the angels don't bust through the windows and pop my head off like a Ken doll.

Then it hits me. Angels wouldn't knock.

Unless they were really, really stupid angels...or it was some kind of diversion. One guy knocks at the front, and the rest swarm the back. Now I'm kind of curious. I still don't have a gun, but I make my way to the front door anyway. I bet they take one look at me and think they have the wrong house. If they expect a mean, lean, angel-killing vigilante, they are in for a big helping of disappointment.

I have my hand on the knob when the knock repeats.

Soft knock. Small hands.

"Shiiiiiiiit," I groan as I swing open the door – brain too slow to react.

On the other end stands an angel, but not the genetically mutated freaks that I kill. Francesca is the real kind of angel, the kind that God spent a little extra time on. That face. Those big brown eyes and sensual mouth. A river of black hair runs down her back. I'd drown in that river if she'd let me. Oh God, I've lavished hours imaging those eyes full of lust and love, those lips pursed waiting to lock onto mine.

*I could make you laugh, Francesca,* I think stupidly. *You'd never stop.*

Her eyes are filled with kindness and warmth...and pity. I imagine her giving that same gentle look to a kid with brain cancer or a poodle with one of those cones around its head that keeps it from licking its stiches.

I almost say, "Bongiorno," but catch my tongue. Instead, I lean against the door and stare at her. *Beautiful.* In the back of my head, I try to remember the last time I took a shower.

"Bongiorno," Francesca says. Her mouth turns up into a hesitant smile.

My heart actually hurts. When I got drained, Maya and Tarren took my mostly-dead carcass to Dr. Lee's cabin, two miles away from our house. It was an understandable decision. My dad saved Dr. Lee from the angels way back, so he knows the whole story and was probably the only person on the planet capable of saving my life. Fact is, he'd been preparing for this sort of thing for a long time and was prepped and ready to drag my ass from the gates of Hell.

That would have been fine. Dr. Lee is like my second father.

He's set my bones, brought down my fevers, and stitched up that one minor gunshot wound. But Francesca is Dr. Lee's housekeeper, and she's going to nursing school on top of that. When they brought me in, Dr. Lee wasn't the only who treated me...the only one who...God, it still makes me want to throw up.

I realize I haven't said anything.

"Yeah?"

The hesitant smile disappears. "I just wanted to see how..."

"I'm fine."

I want this to be over. I want to stop thinking about Francesca sponge bathing my sunken chest and limp dick while I was in the coma the way she would any other drooling vegetable. More than anything, I want those warm, platonically caring eyes to just go away.

"Your hair is shorter," she says, her Italian accent turning even common words into something special, sexy. *Those lips.*

"I cut it." My hand does a quick tour of my bristled scalp. Dr. Lee shaved me quite the bald spot when he put in the staples for the skull fracture. I figured I would look at least marginally less pathetic if I buzzed the rest of my hair off to keep it even. It hasn't really grown back much.

"Have you been...," Francesca starts.

"I'm fine," I say again. I sound angry. I am angry. Not at her, but it comes off that way, and I don't take it back. Let me be the asshole if she will just take that hesitant smile back home with her.

*I love you. Go away. Please go away*

"Tarren and Maya are...gone?"

I almost say, "Strip club," but manage to cough out,

"Business."

I'm still leaning in the doorway, blocking it actually. God, I have all these stupid visions of us married. Not even the wedding or the honeymoon. Just the two of us in our own little cabin in the woods sitting on a porch swing together. She'll be lying on her back, her head in my lap, and I'll lean down knowing those lips are mine. My heart feels like it's going to explode right here. Not so nice after all the work Francesca did to keep me alive.

Francesca's talking. Reminding me about protein shakes and resting whenever I'm tired, and all the crap that Maya won't let up about on the few occasions she's been around. My face must tell Francesca how much I am absolutely hating this, because her words sputter to a stop.

"Thanks, I'll remember that," I say in a flat tone.

"Gabe," she says, "I just want...

"To help. I know. Well, you've helped. I'm still breathing."

Francesca is uncertain. I could close the door right now and make it epically clear, but I won't do that. Not even now when I'd probably saw off my own foot if it would get her to stop looking at me with so much pity.

"Okay," Francesca sighs.

Something stirs below, and honestly it's a relief. Not a lot of activity down there recently. I'd begun to wonder if not all of me woke up from the coma.

"Bye," I choke out and close the door.

Francesca doesn't say anything, just bows her head a little as the door swings. When it closes, I just go down, sliding to the floor. She's out there, mere inches of wooden door away. And yet I couldn't find the love I want in her eyes if I hijacked the

Starship Enterprise and went through a thousand wormholes.

It's better this way. She's safer. That's what matters.

Damn, I need to get high. Like right now. And I need to shoot at something.

# Chapter 2

"You think you can take me?" I squint at the soup cans that hang from the branches in the woods behind our house. Each wears a little hat of snow. Today I picture them as seedy western outlaws sporting crusty cowboy hats and grinning at me with mouths full of rotting teeth.

I grip my Beretta, which I found buried in the couch cushions in the living room. The outlaw leader guffaws, underestimating me. A lethal mistake as many other soup cans have discovered.

"You ain't got the guts!" he sneers. "I thinks yer yellah." His posse laughs with him.

"That the best insult you got?" I reply and take a long drag of the blunt in my left hand. I hold in the smoke, hoping it will soak in and help douse the ache in my ribs. Dr. Lee says I fractured two and cracked one, all on the right side. Nothing to be done about them except keep them taped up and let time do its work. After three months I'm thinking time called into the office with a big *sayonara* and went to live on a commune in Minnesota.

When my lungs begin to burn, I exhale and shoot. Each

recoil slams up my arm, throwing the shots wild and echoing in my tender ribs. I empty the clip. The last bullet nicks the can, and it swings drunkenly on its string.

Only a flesh wound. The outlaw shakes his head in disappointment.

"Fuck me," I mutter. Give me a pink dress and call me Sally. Time was, I could put a bullet through every can out here. From the deepest fiber of my soul, I knew how to shoot, how to absorb the recoil, how to get that bullet where it needed to go.

The ache in my arms and shoulders is like a heartbeat. More ammo. I need more ammo, more practice, and I should probably dredge up some earplugs. I turn around and see Maya leaning against the back door.

Of bloody course she came home just in time to see my little display of complete ineptitude. And she's looking at me with that face again, her big blue-gray eyes all sad and feely.

"Hey," I mutter as I exhale another lungful.

"Hey," she says back.

I don't know why, but it always surprises me how small my sister is. As she stands up proper, she can't be taller than 5'3 or weigh a drop over 120. But that Munchkinitis doesn't mean she's not an ass kicker of epic proportions. Girl could probably put her fist through a car door and then pick it up and throw it at you.

Just a few of the bennies of getting infected and turned into a hybrid angel.

Fate gave Maya a pretty shit deal on that front. Up until six months ago she was a normal human college student, posting weird Facebook updates that were part philosophy, part sarcasm, going to class, and not partying nearly enough. She had a boyfriend. She had a life. And because I was too slow, she lost it all, even her humanity. I think if I did a good deed every single hour of every single day for the rest of my pathetic life, I still wouldn't be able to make up for that epic fail. For letting down the only sister I have left.

Maya's abilities are damn cool, but they didn't exactly come free of charge. I can't help but glance at her gloved hands. The hunger is something she has to constantly control, and the energy sucking thing...I hate thinking about that. Thank the Lord that she's not a full angel. Otherwise I'm not sure if we would be able to help her keep the hunger under control.

I realize that no one's said anything for a full minute. The cold digs through all the layers of my clothes and injects ice into my bones. And Maya won't get that look off her face.

"You're doing it again," I tell her and hit the safety on my gun automatically, even though the clip is empty.

"Doing what?"

"Looking at me like that."

"No I'm not," she huffs. "Like what?"

I almost laugh. She looks so much like Tarren when she frowns, the way her eyes crinkle and her mouth gets tight.

I shrug. "I don't know, like you want to put me in a bubble and feed me chicken soup all day long."

That frown sets a little deeper, and she reaches up to tuck some strands of reddish brown hair behind her ear. It's getting long, the ends touching her shoulders.

"How have you been eating?" she asks.

Yep, here we go with the nanny routine. I walk past her into the house to get out of the cold. I need to play nice. I know that. Maya cares. That's a good thing.

"So, how were the strip clubs?" I ask as I drop carefully onto the couch. My ribs don't take too kindly to the movement, but I manage not to wince like a sissy.

"Dirty, depressing," Maya says. I don't know if she's talking about the strip clubs or the house as her eyes take a tour of the room and her nose wrinkles up in displeasure.

Right, I haven't exactly been Mr. Clean these past few weeks they've been gone. Actually, I think I've been Mr. Clean's evil duplicate from an alternate universe. Just need the goatee.

"Damn," I tell her, "God hates me. You have any idea how long I've been waiting for a mission that involves strip clubs?" I think longingly of all the gyrating female flesh that I missed.

"It was gross," Maya replies. "Most of them were total sinkholes."

"Now you're just rubbing it in," I groan. The shittier the club, the more amenable the women. You'd be amazed at how attentive an over-the-hill stripper can be when you treat her nice. She'll teach you things the *Kama Sutra* wouldn't dare publish.

Maya is quiet. I follow her gaze to the small, brown pine tree that she dragged out of the forest last month. She'd even strung up some lines of popcorn to try and turn it into a Christmas tree.

It was a nice thought, but we haven't done the Christmas thing ever since Mom got sick. Tarren is against celebrating of any kind, and me, I don't know. Mom died in December. So did Tammy. After that, all the fake cheer of Christmas carols always seemed mocking. Plus, it's not like we had anyone but each other to share the holiday with, and Tarren has so little Christmas cheer that Ebenezer Scrooge would consider him a buzzkill.

The tree is sad as piss. All its needles are brown from the water I never gave it. Some cling on, but most have found their way onto the carpet. I need to throw it out. I've had this thought probably a hundred times. I can't stand looking at it, but here it still is. Alone. Abandoned. Shriveling.

Which reminds me... I stamp out my blunt on the coffee table mostly just to be an ass. "So, I see that Tarren's found another excuse not to be here," I mention casually.

Maya turns to me the moment I open my mouth. The speed and grace of her movements sometime remind me of a cat. It's in these tiny ways, almost too fast for the eye to see, that I realize again and again that she's different. Something beyond human.

"He left. He...just left," she says and then launches into a bizarre story of a phone call, a mysterious voice on the other end asking for Tarren by name, and Tarren's response, which was pretty much to take our medical kit and walk off into the sunset on a secretive solo adventure.

I lean back on the couch, careful with my ribs. Wow, Tarren lied about something and then left. Color me shocked. And I haven't even received a cheerful postcard from him yet. What is the world coming to?

Maya gnaws on her lip, and I bring myself back to reality. She's right. It's weird. Definitely weird. Tarren doesn't know anybody. He doesn't have friends except for that piss ant Lo, and Dr. Lee, of course. Could he have found a girlfriend? God, I hope so. A man just shouldn't go dry for that long. It's not right or healthy. If I had his movie star looks you can bet your ass I'd put them to way better use than Tarren ever does.

I know the girlfriend idea is wishful thinking. The scars. Tarren won't even acknowledge them, as if he could just think them out of existence. I swear he'd insist on wearing long-sleeves and pants into hell rather than let anyone see the scars. Trying to talk to him about them is about as pleasant and productive as walking repeatedly into a brick wall.

And he took the medical kit. Not exactly a bouquet of roses.

Maya looks at me in expectation, like this is some kind of Nancy Drew mystery that we can solve together with a magnifying glass and some gumption. I turn off my worry spout. Tarren can take care of himself, and if the situation were dangerous he would have loaded up with weapons and ammo. I tell Maya as much.

Maya starts going on about tracking him down, but I put the kibosh on that.

"Tarren leaves. That's what he does. Get used to it," I tell her.

Maya used to be president of the Tarren-is-an-unfeeling-husk club, but lately it seems like she's given up her membership. With all the time she's spending on the road with him, I think Stockholm Syndrome is starting to set in.

"He's just..." she answers meekly.

"What?" I didn't realize how pissed I was getting until this word snaps out of me. I guess we're doing this. "He's what, Maya? Just Tarren? Yeah, I know." Not like I haven't been living with the guy my entire life. And now I'm thinking about Mom and her cancer again.

I don't want to be in this conversation anymore, so I get up and head for the stairs. I don't want Maya feeling sorry for

Tarren. He and Tammy left back then too, when Mom was sick. The mission. Always the damn mission, but that was just a pathetic excuse. They were afraid of Mom, of all that pain and sickness. And I was just peachy with it? Like watching Mom die wasn't as lovely as having my soul peeled away with a rusted spoon? I tell this to Maya as I walk up the stairs. And yeah, those stairs suck ass, but I don't stop, and I sure as hell don't lean on the bannister, not while Maya's watching.

I tell Maya about how I took care of Mom, how I called Tarren and Tammy when I knew she was dying. How they didn't make it back in time. I don't tell Maya how Mom got so small it seemed like she was just evaporating right in front of my eyes. How all that strength, all that power that had infused her entire being just faded away. It was a good lesson. Anyone can be weak. Anyone can break no matter how strong they pretend to be on the outside.

I get to the top of the stairs, and honestly, I'm pretty much out of strength. I need to go lights out for a few hours, stop thinking about the brother who can't stand to look at me.

"He'd run into a burning building for any one of us," I say, knowing that Maya can hear me with her super ears. "Hell, he'd do it for a complete stranger, but that doesn't make him brave."

Pretty damn good. Didn't even practice it. I slam my bedroom door for emphasis, and it's all I can do to get to the bed before the exhaustion knocks me out like a cartoon mallet.

# *Chapter 3*

The forced shut down does me good. When I wake up from my extended nap, I find Sir Hopsalot settled next to my hip. His nose trembles, and he looks at me with wide, knowing eyes. I reach out and stroke my rabbit's soft gray fur. It only takes three strokes before he's making a happy chewing noise with his back teeth.

Sir Hopsalot is the best. Period. Sure, as sidekicks go, he can't do much heavy lifting and tends to hide under the bed in response to loud noises, but I'd choose him over a Robin or Speedy any day.

As I pet Sir Hopsalot, I decide that I'm going on the next mission. I don't give two shits what Maya and Tarren say. I can withstand Maya's big weepy eyes. Tarren will spew out all this logic about how I'm a liability and angels will descend upon me like a wounded baby deer. Just words. I've been pissing Tarren off since the day I was born. No reason to stop now.

So my hand-to-hand combat is a little rusty, and I can't exactly sprint across a whole city anymore. No biggie. I can still do plenty, like play lookout, take sniper duty, or flash my pretty smile as angel bait. I'm great at angel bait. Course, I can't really start humming the theme music if we don't have a mission.

"Got to find some angels," I tell Sir Hopsalot.

When I sit up, he jumps down from the bed and hops into the big hay bin in the corner of my room. He starts munching his heart out on hay. Little guy loves the stuff. I tried it once and honestly wasn't too impressed. Slap me down a juicy steak and a couple shots of whiskey over hay any day.

I flip open Starbuck, and my beautiful girl hums in greeting as I put in her password. She may not look like much on the outside, but below the hood, I've upgraded my laptop with the latest cache, a processing speed so high it might break the sound barrier, and enough memory to make tomorrow's gamer drool. Oh, and the hard drive is practically big enough to park a school bus. In other words, Starbuck is the shit, which is a good thing since finding angels is pretty much the most important part of the mission, not that you'd get Tarren to admit that even if you pulled out all his fingernails under torture. It's all cool to go stalking the night for justice and take the kill shot, but day-saving doesn't happen without solid detective work first, and that's what I do.

Starbuck and I get to work. I've got Google alerts set up to send me obituaries from all across the country. They filter into my database, and my algorithm runs through them, prying secrets from the dead. The equation is simple, if people under 50 in close proximity to one another start dropping dead of heart attacks, they get flagged. Then it's all about finding a pattern, looking for dark fingerprints across the maps. If the police report mentions a crazy low body temp at time of death, then I win the bad guy lottery. Classic signs of an angel attack. Heart gives out from the stress of the energy drain and body heat gets zapped away.

Problem.

The angels don't want to come out and play today. I follow body after body and come up with nothing but a lot of natural causes or trails that are stretched and faint. Hardly enough to go galloping after, guns brandished. After an hour, my brain starts to hurt and my thoughts keep wandering away like bored kittens. I have to tear my eyes from the screen, breathe, and then go about collecting all those damn kittens again. This is bad. I've always been a little ADHD...okay, maybe more than a little, but my brain and I have been a good team. I should be able to go hiking through the internet for hours, but now sixty minutes seems to have eaten through my entire supply of concentration. Another shiny present from the Head Injury Express.

And what's with the angel no-show? Honestly, it's become an all-you-can-eat bad guy buffet these past couple of years. As their numbers grow, their discipline is going down the toilet. In the good old days, the angels were careful with their kills, made me work to find them. Nowadays, you've got Special Olympic rejects running all over the place just leaving bodies in their wake like it ain't no thang.

Course, I say that, and look who has nothing to show so far.

The universe is mocking me.

Well, the universe doesn't fucking know me very well, because I get knocked down on my ass plenty, but so far I've always gotten back up. If the victims won't lead me to any angels, then I'll find them a different way.

I fall back down on my bed, listen to Starbuck hum, and look to Keira Knightly for support. Her eyes smolder from the poster above my bed, and she certainly gives me a lot to think about…just not anything related to my cerebral territory.

Okay, change of tactics.

I look out the window and let my mind wander down a thousand unrelated alleys. I wonder where the hell Tarren's gone and why he doesn't trust Maya and me with his secrets. Does he think he could do anything that I wouldn't forgive or understand? Come on, we kill people. Not like I've got much moral high ground here.

My thoughts swing to Tammy. My sister loved the snow. That was her way. What everyone else hated, she loved — spiders, snakes, the loudest, screamiest rock music. Everything about her was loud. She could laugh so hard, especially if it was at your expense, that you felt like the earth was shaking under your feet. But there was no way of staying mad at her. I always thought she could charm the Grim Reaper into giving her a second shot at life.

I was wrong.

Tammy would have thought this gray, cold, ugly day was beautiful. She would have revved her motorcycle and sped off to go find a blizzard to dance in.

*Blizzard.* I sit up. Sir Hopsalot pauses in his hay gorge-fest for a moment and then resumes his loud chewing.

"Blizzards," I say to him and laugh. "Blizzards, blizzards, blizzards!"

The rest of the day is a blur. Starbuck and I get epic together. The internet is our bitch as we pull up news on major weather events and I lay out all the resulting corpses for review. I'm onto something. I can feel it. Bad guys, come out, come out wherever you are….

Maya returns with bags of groceries. I didn't even notice her leave. Technically, according to the rules of the All-Knowing-Tarren, she's not supposed to go out on her own without one of us chaperoning in case she goes all Godzilla on the innocents of Farewell, Colorado. Tarren is paranoid as a meth addict when it comes to Maya. I think if they made those child bungee leashes in adult sizes, he would strap her in and never let her out.

Tarren is wrong about Maya. As wrong as anyone could be about anything. The sky will turn red, Scooby will get tired of Scooby snacks, Tarren will get a sense of humor before Maya hurts an innocent person. I see the scary cold need in her eyes sometimes, but she can control it. She won't go dark side. She just won't.

My sister sets food besides me as I work, protein shakes, sandwiches, badly-cooked pasta. I'm pissed that we're back to the nanny routine, but I'm also hungrier than a Hungry, Hungry Hippo. So I basically inhale the food, and somewhere along the way, the plates disappear.

She drags me away from the computer that night, asking if I want to play some video games. I pretend like I've played them all to death, but the truth is I can hardly beat them anymore, even on the easy setting. My reflexes are shot, and after a few levels, my concentration goes all wandering kittens again. Instead, we watch the original *RoboCop* from my DVD collection. I don't even think I make it halfway through before I'm conked out for the night. Pathetic me.

I wake up the next morning with a pillow under my head and a blanket over my shoulders. Sweet sister. Still no dreams. Maybe that's a good thing. The house is silent, and it must be early, because only a hint of light plays beneath the window blinds. I sit up and wait for the aches and pains to start knocking, but I actually feel good today. Or at least better. Probably what happens when I'm not left in charge of feeding myself.

I blink and realize something is different. I sit up and look around for honestly a full minute before I realize the fugly Christmas tree is gone. So are all the empty beer bottles and dirty plates on the coffee table. My deluge of DVDs has disappeared, probably stacked neatly in the entertainment center.

In a word, the house no longer needs a hazmat unit to come out and do a controlled demolition for the safety of the community. Just one more benefit of a hybrid angel in the family – she has a lot of energy and doesn't need much sleep.

For the first time in a long time, the thought of a shower actually crosses my mind, but I have more important work to do. I feed Sir Hopsalot and then pet Starbuck as I boot her up. When she's awake and ready to get ass kicking, I put her into the port on my desk in the dining room where I've got three monitors lined up. I already know what I've found, but now it's time to track the fuckers, see if I can pinpoint their next move. Sir Hopsalot jumps into my lap and settles over my legs just as the front door opens.

"I cleaned all your clothes yesterday," Maya says behind me. "When's the last time you changed?"

I lean back in my chair and glance at my sister. Her hair bounces in a short ponytail with lots of little wisps sticking out. Maya's got a touch of pink in both cheeks, which means she's probably just returned from bounding around the woods like a gazelle on steroids.

"What's today?" I ask her.

Her mouth turns down, the same way Tarren's does. Stockholm all the way. "Did you eat breakfast?"

Yep, here we go. "Thanks for cleaning everything," I tell her. It's mostly sincere, but I really want her to ditch the worry eyes. "Must have taken you all night."

Maya gives me a look that says a lot of things I really don't want to hear. She's disappointed, of course. A monkey could'a taken better care of this place than me. I know that. All she says out loud though is, "Then it's a good thing that I don't need much sleep."

She looks up at the collection of action figures on the shelf above my computer monitors. More mouth turning down. More disappointed nose scrunch.

I'm pretty proud of the scene, actually. I'd found some Jonas brother action figures at a garage sale in Fresno last year, and they're currently being pounded into the ground by Conan, while Rogue stomps green army men. Mr. Incredible has lost his left arm, but he fights on against a tag-team of Chun Li and a Cylon.

Maya wants to know what happened. I remember coming home after the whole coma episode to find all my action figures standing together, no weapons, no missing limbs. I could practically hear them singing *We Are The World* together. It was a nice thought, something only Maya would have done.

"Peace never lasts," I tell her.

"A shame," she says, and her voice is way too serious for a conversation about over-muscled plastic dolls. "Have you eaten?"

She's like a bloodhound. "Yeah. So, I think I've found some angel activity."

Maya is already in the kitchen. I hear the fridge open.

Damn her. "I think you're going to be really impressed," I call after her. "This was some good detective work on my part."

"Noted," she calls back. I hear her opening the cabinets, pulling out dishes.

As she works, I start setting up the big reveal. "So what's the number one difficulty angels face?" I ask.

After a slight pause, Maya answers, "Controlling the hunger."

"Okay, there's that," I admit, "but since all angels pretty much fail 'Not Killing People 101,' what I..."

"Oh really."

Jesus! Maya is just behind me. I didn't even hear her footsteps. She lays a plate of food beside me along with a protein shake. I make a face at it.

"I mean in general," I tell her. "As a hybrid, you're the exception of course."

"Of course."

I give her a quick glance to make sure she's not pissed. Maya's face is still, but something is going on with her eyes. Just for a moment, I get a sense of that other part of her. The angel part. All hungry and animal. I turn quickly back to the computer screen. This happens sometimes with her. It's best to ignore it.

"Getting caught was the answer I was looking for," I say and show her my lovely Google maps filled with the shining brilliance of my detective work. She leans over to look, and I can tell she's impressed. After a little more back and forth, I point to the map.

"I noticed a cluster of deaths in the Midwest. Missouri and Illinois this past week."

Maya puts a hand on her hip and plays right along. "What does this have to do with getting caught?"

*Ding, ding, ding, we have a winner!*

"Weather," I announce proudly.

"Weather?"

"The Midwest is getting bent over and spanked by the mother of all ice storms. There's power outages, cancelled schools, airport pandemonium."

Maya catches on. "People are stuck in their homes."

"Exactly. Confusion. Chaos. It's the perfect killing ground." I give her details about the patterns I found going years back. Bodies showing up after hurricanes, power outages, even tornados.

Maya cuts right to the chase. "You think we're looking for multiple wings?"

I scratch Sir Hopsalot behind his floppy ear. "Lots of bodies," I tell her.

"Are you sure we're even dealing with angels?"

"Nope. No way to be sure until we check it out." I suck in my breath.

"We?"

"I already have a bag packed. Let me know when you're ready." That's a lie, but she doesn't need to know that. Maya gives me a look that says, *There is no way in the seven hells you are going on the mission with us.*

*Yeah, but what are you going to do to stop me?* I think back.

Maya opens her mouth, and I expect a barrage of

arguments. "So, did you ever find anything out about The Totem, or whatever, that group who posted that YouTube video?"

Geez, non-sequitur much? I think back to the craptastic home video I dug up two months ago. Besides being good for a laugh, it wasn't worth sweating over. Basically a bunch of Losers, capital L, decided to throw on some cheap animal masks and tell the world about angels via YouTube. It was obvious that they'd had some kind of encounter with the enemy, but half the details were wrong. Amateurs. No, that's too kind. Butt-faced amateurs who are going to get their legs torn off and their masks shoved into very small orifices if they manage to accidentally come across any more angels.

"Even if they manage to stumble across an angel, they'll get dead real fast, problem solved," I tell my sister.

"Serves them right," Maya agrees, but her eyes have gone all distant. She's been weird about that video from the first time she saw it. Probably worried about the poor dopes. As far as I'm concerned they're digging their own graves. Not much to be done except to step back and try to avoid any flying intestines.

"So, we should start getting ready," I tell Maya. It's about fucking time for my triumphant comeback.

# Chapter 4

Maya calls Tarren with my great and wonderful news that there might be more people for him to kill. I sit on the couch smoking a joint and dropping in helpful commentary throughout the entire call. Tarren must ask how I'm doing, because Maya looks at me and questions, "How are you?"

I give her a big smile dripping in sarcasm. "Tell Tarren that I died. See what he does. You think he'd let you take the time to bury me before you left, or would he just tell you to stuff my body in the freezer until after the mission?"

Maya's eyes grow cold, and her body tenses. "He's being a complete asshole," she reports to my brother. Oh yeah? You want asshole? Guess exactly how many times Tarren has called to make sure I was still breathing? That would be exactly zero.

I'm obviously a sucker for family dysfunction 'cause I keep up with the snide remarks. By the end of the call Maya is more pissed at me than I think I've ever seen her. To be honest I prefer pissed to pitying. At least she's treating me like a real person.

"Bet he didn't even say goodbye," I tell her when she hangs up.

That does it. Maya whirls around and snatches the blunt out of my mouth so fast that I hardly see her hand move. She snuffs it out in the new ashtray that appeared on the coffee table this morning.

"What the fuck?" I tell her. "That's for medicinal purposes."

"Don't be mean about Tarren," she yells back, seething with full-on rage. Of course Maya would stand up for Tarren. Clearly that emotionless hulk is the victim in this entire encounter. I'm ready to scream and shout, so that's exactly what I do.

"Yeah?" I tell her. "Why not? He doesn't even act human." I mean who just runs away when his brother is in a coma? If it were the other way around, I swear I wouldn't leave his bedside. I'd piss in a bucket if I had to. I'd give him anything, blood, bone marrow, kidneys, my idiot heart.

And he ran away.

"You have no idea how much he cares," Maya whispers. "What he was like when you got hurt."

She drops her head, and damn, her face is haunted. What in the hell happened between them when I went all coma sleepy time? What did Tarren do? I've always worried about the way he pents up all his emotions. He's liable to blow a gasket one of these days. Maybe he did. That thought acts like a needle, popping the expanding anger in my chest.

"I know," I tell her. She doesn't say anything, just turns around and goes up to her room, probably to pack. I guess I deserve the cold shoulder. When did things get so tangled between us? I try to think of the last time we spent half a night up on the roof gazing at the stars and talking about anything other than the mission or the old life she lost.

I head up to my room and pack. The process feels good, like I'm finally doing something that matters. I pull open drawers and throw in stacks of long underwear and the fitted black shirts and pants that cost a small fortune at REI. The stuff is flexible, rain resistant, tough as nails, and also looks hell-a good, if I say so myself. Totally worth the Godzilla-sized price tag. I find two Berettas placed side by side on my dresser. I wonder what nooks and crannies Maya found them in during her cleaning spree. I throw the heat in my bag along with some extra mags and an armful of vitamin bottles that Dr. Lee gave to me. If I'm going to be day-saving again, I need to get back up to full strength ASAP. By the time I'm ready, my duffle bag looks like it's been hitting Old Town Buffet like a bad crack habit. I just need to remember to grab the case of lettuce mix Sir Hospalot likes.

Speaking of my sidekick, I find him flopped on his side and passed out on the floor next to my awesome bean bag chair. His head jerks up when I sit down next to him. I give his soft fur some strokes then put him in his carrying case. I bring my bags to the garage and watch with amusement as Maya checks the tire pressure on the shiny black jeep that somehow replaced our Murano SUV a few months back. She tops off the oil and goes over the contents of the back about twenty times.

This is her first run at gearing up for a mission, and she's being all perfectionist about it. Her small face scrunches up in concentration, and those pale blue eyes seem to dart all over the place looking for even the tiniest imperfection. It's crazy cold in the garage, enough to turn a dribble of spit into an icicle before it hits the ground, but Maya hardly seems to notice in her tight jeans and plain gray long-sleeve shirt. After another lookover of the back, she tears off a big sheet of tarp, folds it up, and adds it to the supplies.

Finally, she looks at me. Her eyes travel over the bags at my feet and her expression turns all sad and pitying. Then she notices the keys to the jeep in my hand. I snagged them this morning as a well-considered precaution.

My sister sighs, just the way Mom used to. I can't help but smile remembering how many of those same sighs I rung out of our mother. Not as many as Tammy managed, but who could ever compete with Tammy when it came to anything, especially annoying the hell out of Mom?

"I could just hotwire the jeep," Maya says.

Damn, probably shouldn't have taught her how to do that. "Yeah and Tarren would be really happy about that," I answer her.

Maya looks so small right now, just like the frazzled college girl she's supposed to be. I realize for the millionth time how much I hate that she's going on missions and putting herself in danger. I'd hoped that after she sent Grand packing to hell *(Don't let the ebony gates of eternal torture hit your ass on the way in)* she wouldn't want to hunt wings anymore. But I'm starting to realize that she's got too much of Tarren in her. He's infected her with the mission. The stupid, wretched mission. I'm all for killing bad guys, but Tarren and Maya treat it like a sacred duty handed down from Heaven. That means I have to look out for them, make sure they don't hand their souls over for one extra kill.

"I want to go this time," I tell her. "I can handle it, I swear." I give Maya my biggest, saddest puppy dog eyes. These babies literally got me out of jail once.

Her face hardens. "No."

"Why not?" Anger churns up inside me, all hot and volatile just like when Tammy and I used to have our spectacular fights. Maya looks at me, and her doubts are all over her face. She thinks I'm weak, a liability. Without a word, she hits a button on the wall, and the garage door rumbles to life. The cold attacks like a bloodhound. Maya walks past me to the work bench and lifts off a roll of duct tape.

Oh this is going to be good.

"What, you going to duct tape me to a chair or something?"

Maya turns and walks toward me. Her face is scary cold. For the first time, I realize that she could be capable of anything. Killing Grand changed her, and all this buddy-buddy time with Tarren isn't doing her any favors in the soft and cuddly department. I don't like this hardened version of my sister.

Maya reaches for me, and I have to force myself not to flinch. In a blur, she tugs my lucky hat off my head. I grope for it, but she's too fast. Now she runs out of the garage straight for the big maple tree in the front yard.

That tree. Of course that fucking tree. It's been my lifelong arch-nemesis ever since Tammy tied me to its trunk for an entire night using jump ropes when we were kids. An endless night of getting eaten by mosquitoes while my dislocated shoulder throbbed in agony and I waited for the inevitable moment when a huge grizzly would rear out of the forest and tear my head off.

"Oh come on!" I call to Maya as she leaps into the tree and

bounds up the branches like a goddamned monkey. Her stellar acrobatics would be impressive if she weren't holding my lucky hat hostage. She moves like she's got feathers for bones, that dark ponytail swinging up and down with each leap. In less than thirty seconds, she's halfway up the tree. The tape comes out, and my lucky hat gets a duct tape bath as she secures it to a branch.

I groan. We've already done this dance before. She taped my hat to the very top branch of the evil tree last year as a practical joke, but I turned the tables on her when I climbed my ass up there and got it back. I still remember the look on her face when I brought the hat down. The forces of good prevailed that day.

I wrap my arms around my chest, but it does nothing to keep out the cold. It'd seemed so easy back then to get up those branches. All instinct. I've been climbing trees and fences and scrambling onto roofs my whole life. Now, the distance looks intimidating. Can trees gloat?

Once my poor hat is secured, Maya leaps out of the tree, arching into a perfect backflip.

"Cute," I tell her and run a hand through my short, prickly hair. I look up at my hat. It was my dad's, the only thing I have of his. Mom used to tell me I was his spitting image, but I've spent hours gazing at the few pictures we have left and I don't see it. My dad is strong, confident, and handsome. Mom said he had a great sense of humor before he became an angel hunter.

I pull my eyes away from the hat and look at Maya. "You think I won't go just cause I don't have my hat?"

Maya's playing at something. Her face is a mask. "If you get it, I'll let you come on the mission. Not a day sooner."

"Really?" The wind doesn't feel so cold. I glance up at the hat. It's only half way up the tree. Only half way.

"No cheating," Maya says.

I can get it. I know I can. This tree is my bitch.

"Fine," I tell her. I set my bags down in the garage, shrug out of my coat, and stare at my nemesis.

There comes a time in every comic book arc where the villain beats the superhero into a bloody pile of splintered bones, punctured organs, and crapped pants. Our hero isn't just down and out, he is ass whupped, and the villain is tearing the entire world apart around his pulped carcass and probably fondling his girlfriend too. Any other person would give up and sulk off to a corner to die, but the hero – because he's a superhero and this is what they do – stands up one more time and finds a way to win the day.

This is my moment. I'm going to do it. Doesn't matter how. It's gonna happen, because I've got to protect Maya and make sure Tarren actually sleeps. I've got to get out of this claustrophobic house.

I run at that tree, every step powerful with promise. I hardly feel the aches in my knees, the fingers of cold in my bones. I leap, and my arms find the first branch.

My ribs explode with pain, but none of that matters. I've just got to get up and around. My momentum carries me over...almost. Right at the apex of the swing, I slow and come back down.

No way in hell I'm letting go of this branch. Not ever. My ribs are weeping, but I pull my legs up. I hang upside down, bear hugging the lowest branch. There's got to be a way.

This. Is. My. Fucking. Moment.

My hands begin to slide. *DON'T,* I warn them. *DON'T YOU DARE YOU MOTHERFUCKERS.*

Then I'm falling, hitting the ground. Maya's there, her hands on my back to keep me from putting my ass in the snow.

"Get away!" I tear myself from her touch. My body screams at me in a hundred different directions, but it doesn't compare to what's happening in my chest. My heart cringes.

Maya stands next to me, and her face is artic cold. I'm losing her. I can feel it.

"Give me the keys," she says in a hard voice.

*Go fish!* I heave the keys into the woods, but they don't go far. *Pathetic.*

"Classy," Maya says.

"Have fun, don't get dead," I retort back. I grab my stuff and stomp to the house.

"Gabe, wait."

I turn around, hoping against hope that she's changed her mind, that she'll crack a smile and be the sweet sister she was before I made a disaster of everything.

"It's because we care, because we love you."

And isn't that the biggest load of bullshit the planet has ever known.

"No, it's not love." I stare at her. It's so obvious. "I know what it really is. I can see it in your face."

Maya's mouth tightens. Her eyes are a pale blue. They change color sometimes almost to a smoky gray. Tarren's eyes do the same thing. "What? What do you see?" she asks.

"Pity." I slam the door to the garage, leaving her to the snow and the cold.

## *Chapter 5*

I try some Tai' Chi to calm myself down, but my brain is running as fast as a roided-out, supremely pissed hamster on a wheel. After half an hour I give up on the energy flow and drown my sorrows the old-fashioned way, with the rest of the beer in the fridge and then the bottle of Jack I keep hidden in the back of my closet.

It doesn't take much alcohol anymore before things start feeling better and the room decides to sway, but I figure it won't hurt anything to keep piling on the shots. Somewhere along the way it becomes a great idea to strip down to my boxers and sing the songs on my angel hunting soundtracks at the top of my lungs. I holler out *Highway to Hell, This is the Danger Zone,* and *Going the Distance*, among other classics and impress the hell out of my action figures with my mad dance moves. I'm pretty sure they start cheering at some point.

Later on, after the dancing, Sir Hopsalot and I have a really powerful bro sesh. I basically pour my heart out to him, and he is just the best listener in the world. Hands-down. Doesn't judge, doesn't talk over me, doesn't tell me to drink a protein shake. Together we decide that it is imperative that we follow

Maya in the morning and get in on the mission despite her command. What can they do once I'm already there?

It all seems to make perfect, beautiful sense until I wake up the next morning on the floor still a little drunk but mostly hung over so bad I can hardly move. Then I remember how pathetic I am and why Maya and Tarren want me nowhere near a gun.

Life is such a suckfest sometimes.

***

Sometime in the afternoon, I finally sign into *World of Warcraft*, which I haven't done since I went down for the count with the whole coma shindig. My Level 80 Rogue, Apollo, has probably started gnawing off his own leg in boredom.

Over the years I've developed some pretty tight friendships within the game, and my peeps often let me drop into their guilds and fight the good fight even though I'm just a part timer. I've practically been a ghost since last year when the angels hit their Baby Boom and the whole secret-sister-got-turned-into-a-hybrid-angel-whoopsie-daisy bombshell fell. My WOW buddies have all abandoned me by now, so I just walk around and kill a few things on my own and pick up a mission or two that I'll probably never complete. Then, a little message pops up, alerting me that WildStarz2346 is on.

She and I originally met on SecondLife a long time ago, but that show is so over. I brought her over to WOW, and by the looks of her Night Elf Druid, she's not doing too bad for herself. Gotta love a girl with big...balance mojo. I find her avatar and look at that svelte figure wrapped in leather and knee-high boots.

I realize that I want to see her. Not just in the game. I greet her the way I always do.

You got a boyfriend yet?

Long pause on the other end, and I try to remember the last time I dropped in at her place. It's been, *crap-ola*, since before we rescued Maya. I guess in the real world that might come off as a cold shoulder.

Just you, she writes back.

Bingo, Yhatzee and Connect Four!

Mind if I come over? Might as well get to the point.

Another pause. Me feeling more guilty about stagging her for so long.

I've missed you, she finally writes.

Me too. I can explain. I'll be over tonight then.

Bring some whipped cream. WildStarz can be a flirt. Must be those big blue eyes and pointed elf ears. Amanda, the girl behind the elf, is shy as can be. Sweet though. Real sweet.

Conveniently, I'm already packed. I shoulder my duffle bag, as is, and get Sir Hopsalot back into his carrying case. I put everything into the front seat of Bubba, my Ford F-150 and give the hood a nice slap for good luck. Bubba's getting on in years, and he's lost a little paint on various misadventures, but the son-of-a-bitch hasn't let me down yet. As I pull out of the garage, I take a moment to look up longingly at my lucky hat, still up in that Satan tree.

Bad idea going to meet a girl without my lucky hat. I think about giving the tree one more go, but dismiss it. No need for a repeat performance of yesterday's humiliation.

I need to get strong again. If I were honest with myself, I'd admit I've been slacking off on all the instructions Dr. Lee and Francesca left me about guzzling protein shakes every few hours, taking a load of vitamins, and focusing on light cardio. I stare at the hat. Really throw some eye daggers at it. Things are going to change. I'm all in from this moment on. Ready to pack on some muscles. Woo Amanda good and hard. Climb that motherfucking tree like a champ and start saving the holy hell out of the world whether it wants me to or not.

***

Bubba gets me to Denver in a couple of hours, and I manage to pound back three protein shakes on the way. It's amazing how many calories I can put down and still look as weak and skinny as Olive Oil. I hate thinking about that or what Amanda's going to see when I knock on her door.

I like to bring her a little present every time I see her. Nothing fancy. Just a small thank you for not changing the locks, and because I have a feeling that she doesn't get a lot of visitors. These times when we're together are special for me, but I think they're really special to her.

I pull into a little flower shop and greet the shopkeeper, a tiny old lady with hair as white and fluffy as cotton. Definitely somebody's adorable grandma, which is my luck, because I happen to be great with grandmas. A couple of smiles, and a few "pleases" and "ma'ams" later, and Nancy is hopping all around the place, pulling out flowers galore for me. She brings back this bouquet filled with flowers I couldn't name if my life depended on it, but they're beautiful. Citrus orange flowers mix with bright yellow ones and sprigs of white dance around the sides to set it off. The price tag is $49.99.

I haven't gotten around to telling Tarren yet, but we're almost completely broke. So, I pass on the big, beautiful bouquet and go for a handful of lilies instead for $9.99. Nancy, my new best friend, wraps them up for me, and she does a really good job, putting a ribbon around them and this nice clear plastic wrap. I know she's giving me extra even though I bought about the cheapest thing in the store.

While she's doing her magic, a man walks into the store hand-in-hand with a little girl. The girl is stork skinny, all legs and arms topped with wild curly hair. Inside the store, she immediately pulls out of her father's grip and starts touching and tugging on everything. She actually skips. It's real cute.

"What do you think Mom would like?" the dad asks.

"Uhhhhh," the girl says. I can't tell kid ages at all, but she's real young, maybe five or six. "Everything."

"Everything, huh? I don't think we could fit everything in the car. How about you pick out one bouquet. Whatever you think is the most beautiful."

I make sure not to stare, since I'm not really looking to come off as a major creep. It's just that I like this. Normal people doing normal people stuff. I don't get much opportunity to see what the rest of the world is up to with their lives, so when I do, I try to remember it, especially nice people like this father and his little girl. Helps sometimes when we're digging graves in the middle of the night, checking into another forgettable hotel room, or putting 700 miles under our tires in a single day.

I lay the flowers carefully on the front seat of the truck, pull off a leaf, and tuck it into Sir Hopsalot's cage for him to nibble on. Then I stop at WalGreens and buy a bottle of whipped cream and some condoms. Ribbed for her pleasure. I'm a thoughtful kind of guy.

The sun is just setting when I finally snag an empty parking spot in Amanda's apartment complex. I wander around a little until I find her door, the one with the little bluebird welcome sign on the front. I give the door a solid knock and rock back and forth on my feet while I wait. I actually feel nervous. That's never happened before, not with Amanda. I really am losing my touch. God I need my lucky hat.

"Lee!" she cries happily as the door swings open, and it really is good to see her face and that big nervous smile putting dimples in both cheeks. Amanda loves the flowers. The way she cradles them, you'd think they were made out of gold or something. Course, that's before she notices Sir Hopsalot, and then he's the center of attention. My sidekick is pretty shameless about the whole cock blocking thing too. Amanda puts him right down in her lap and strokes his fur, and he just lets her do it. We're definitely going to have a conversation about proper wingman behavior at some point in the near future.

Amanda's shy in person. Doesn't need to be. She's put on a little more weight since I saw her last, but she's still a pretty girl. At least I think so. Her apartment is exactly as I left it. Same little TV sitting on the way too big media center, same hand-me-down coffee table, same faint scent of floral perfume.

It takes her an hour to finally ask about my appearance, though she's been giving me strange eyes since I got here.

"Cancer," I tell her. "Liver."

She actually gasps, and a look of such horror crosses her face that it makes me uncomfortable. "Lee, oh no!"

"It's okay," I tell her quickly, "I'm in remission. Docs are hopeful it won't be back. Though nothing is sure." I tack on that last part, because who knows what could happen in the field. Maybe I'm in the ground next month, and it'd be better if Amanda thought cancer got me rather than that I just dropped her like last night's trash.

The cancer bit works wonders. Sir Hops alot is left out in the cold, and now I'm the one getting petted. I close my eyes, feel Mandy's hands on me, and it's real nice.

***

Amanda sets me up on the couch, finds season three of *Battlestar Galatica* on Netflix, and prepares dinner. I'm not allowed to do anything. I try, but she knows I couldn't peel a carrot if I had a gun to my head, and since I'm a cancer survivor, you know, I get certain bennies.

I half watch the show – seen 'em all at least three times each – and half watch Amanda. The girl is amazing, like a conductor at the center of an orchestra. Three pans sizzle on the stove while she mixes something in a bowl and sets it down to chop up vegetables and sprinkle spices onto a big slab of meat. She doesn't use the microwave, not once.

By the time dinner is ready, I've got a serious case of drool going on. The whole little apartment smells like the kitchen of a five star restaurant, or at least what I think a five star restaurant would smell like. Mandy brings me over to this tiny table stuffed in the corner of the kitchen where plates and silverware wait for us. My lilies cluster together in a glass in the center of the table, between a pair of mismatched candles. She's even set out wine glasses.

I wish she weren't so nervous though, thinking everything

is over cooked or under cooked or there is a little too much ginger in this or that. I have to keep assuring her everything is fine, but it's hard, because I'm stuffing my face like a maniac. I'm sure it's delicious, but chewing isn't so much in my plans.

I think I gross Amanda out a little bit.

"Cancer," I mumble through the food, and she breaks out the sad eyes and nods understandably. Bless cancer.

We watch two more episodes of *Battlestar Galactica*. Amanda leans into me, murmuring how cool it is that my name is Lee, just like the brave, suave, muscled CAG on the show. Ironic indeed.

We go to the bedroom after that. Course I have to run right back out again, because I forgot the whipped cream in the truck. When I bring it in, Amanda laughs all high and nervous. Toes are her thing, so I take off her socks, put a dollop of whip cream on each digit and then suck it off. That really gets her. She throws her head back and starts groaning. I kiss the tops of her feet and the little bony bump at her ankles.

I think about Francesca, like I always do right before I have sex with Amanda or the other girls that I've picked up in bars and other places around the country. But I'm not with Francesca tonight. I'm with Amanda. I take Francesca by her small, warm hands and lead her to the back of my mind. I put her in a lavish bedroom and lay her out on one of those heart shaped beds with crimson silk sheets. I leave her a bottle of wine and make sure the Jacuzzi in the center of the room is going, and then I close the door. I'll come back another night when I'm lonely and when it's not so painful thinking of her taking care of me when I was in a coma.

Amanda puts her hands through my hair.

"I liked it longer," she says.

"I'll grow it back out for you."

"I can't believe you had cancer, Lee," she says. When I look up, she's actually crying about it.

"I'm right here," I say. "I'm okay.

"Lee," she whimpers, "I...I..." Another tear rolls down her face.

"What?"

She turns her face away. "I'm fat," she huffs.

I know exactly how to play this. I lean in and give her a long kiss. "I like the way you look," I say. "If anyone should be self-conscious, it's me."

Truth is I can't stand to look at myself in the mirror anymore. Sometimes I wish I had even a tenth of Tarren's looks. He's got a face meant for the movies and packs on muscles like it's going out of style. Doesn't care a whit about it either. All the girls go ga ga the moment he enters a room with that tortured warrior vibe oozing out of his pores, and the big lug doesn't even notice. The scars. It's hard to be jealous of Tarren and the lot God gave him. I still am though, and it makes me angry as all hell at myself.

"You had cancer," Amanda says. "You have a right to look...different. I just can't stop eating potato chips.

"Come on." I put my hand up her shirt. "I think you look fine. You want to turn the lights down more?"

She nods, so I do. I also doc my iPod in her station and put on a playlist I made for having sex. I call it my "relaxing" playlist, but really it's just for sex. Then, I take my clothes off. All of them. I look like a fifth grader who's about five years away from puberty.

"See," I tell Amanda, "If I can get naked, you can get naked."

Then I crouch. Mandy notices what I'm doing. "Lee, don't!"

I leap into the bed and tackle her with kisses.

Between us, we finish the bottle of whipped cream.

When we're done, I think about putting my clothes back on, but I'm too tired to get out of bed. I ask Amanda about her job and get her to tell me everything that's been going on with her coworkers. She works in the shipping and receiving department of an industrial chemical manufacturer and thinks it's the most boring job in the world. She never believes me when I tell her I want to hear about it. Thinks I'm just trying to win nice guy points. But it's real interesting to me, like catching a glimpse of a foreign planet where things aren't like *drive, drive, drive, watch, watch, watch, BAM!, wrap up the body, get it in the ground – repeat indefinitely*. I press her for the most random details like what's on her desk at work. What kind of forms she has to fill out. What coffee they use in the break room.

She asks me questions, and I tell her about our last software tradeshow, the new update to the programming, and how the economy has slammed us hard. I've got to be careful about what I tell her. Usually, I've got my fake life down pat, names, people, software details, everything. But ever since the coma, I can't remember anything for shit. It's gotten so bad, I actually scribbled down some notes on the way here.

Also, I'm really tired. I can feel sleep pulling me down with metal hooks. Before the draining, I was able to stay up three days straight and hardly feel it. Now, I can barely make it through the day without conking out and sleeping like I'm dead.

Amanda is asking too many questions. I can't remember what my boss's name is supposed to be or if Michigan is in my sales territory or not. My head is starting to throb. So, I just start making up this story about how I rescued the first lady after she was secretly kidnapped by terrorists.

Amanda giggles as I throw in explosions, a galloping horse, and an evil Russian named Ivan. The last thing I remember is me pulling on a parachute and telling the first lady to hold on tight before leaping from a burning helicopter.

Then I'm just gone.

# Chapter 6

Sleep is not something I wake up from anymore. I've got to drag myself out of it, like a pit of mud. I don't dream, or if I do, the dreams hit that damaged part of my brain and disappear into the abyss.

When I finally crank my eyelids open, Mandy's round, purple alarm clock announces that it is 10:23 AM. In those first few seconds, I know it's going to be a migraine day. Amanda pulled the shades down, bless that girl, but even the faint glow of sunlight pierces into my skull. Head movement of any kind is an invite to paintopia.

I put Mandy's pillow over my face and lie there for a good hour feeling real sorry for myself while the pain takes cheap shots right behind my eyes. Never had so much as a headache before the coma, 'cept for that one time this angel released some sort of sonic blast that threw me headfirst into a street lamp when I was seventeen. Tammy and Tarren made me stay awake all night, taking turns walking round and round a high school track with me after we buried that angel. Tammy told me the filthiest jokes I ever heard that night.

What eventually gets me up from Mandy's bed is not courage, not gusto or anything like that. I've got to take the mother of all pisses, and if it were my own bed, I might consider just letting go, but since this is Amanda's pad, I pull myself up and stagger into the bathroom.

My head's so bad I actually have to sit down to pee. Good thing I'm already naked, because I'm not sure I would've remembered to pull my pants down. I never let on with Maya and Tarren how bad the migraines get, but since no one's in the apartment I just let the pathetic all out. This includes actually crawling back to the bedroom instead of walking.

I dive into my bag and can barely get the lid off the meds Dr. Lee gave me. After another hour of lying sprawled on the floor with last night's t-shirt over my eyes, the pain backs off enough so that I'm capable of basic higher level thinking.

When I drag myself back to the bathroom for a shower, I notice in the mirror that I've got a kiss print on my forehead. Amanda always likes to put it there in the morning right after she applies her lipstick. Usually I'm awake to kiss her back. Sweet girl.

The shower is bliss. I probably add a couple grand to Mandy's water bill, that's how long I stay in there, but when I get out, I'm feeling better. My eyes are still half swollen shut, and my head is like an overripe watermelon screwed onto my neck, but at least I'm walking upright.

I take two more pills and wander into the small kitchen. Breakfast is waiting. Scrambled eggs, toast, bacon, and a bowl of oatmeal. A little note from Amanda tells me how long I should heat each thing up in the microwave. Honestly, I almost heave all over the kitchen floor just looking at the stuff. My stomach is in no mood to actually do the whole food thing for probably the next decade. I hate doing this, but I scrape the food off the plate into the trash and throw some wadded up paper towels in after to hide the evidence of my deceit.

Two small bowls sit on the floor next to the table. One contains a few remaining shreds of browning salad mix, the other is filled with water. I find my furry compatriot chillaxing on Amanda's comfy brown couch. The ribbon from my bouquet is tied in a bow around his neck. Mandy probably wouldn't be so pro-rabbit if she'd seen that his little round poops decorate the couch like a handful of raisins.

Yesterday I set up the box of hay that he uses as a litter box in the corner of the living room, but he doesn't use it consistently when we travel. I put my sidekick into the box now and explain the "good guest rules". He listens with his serious face but then hops right out of the box the moment I turn my back to gather up the pellets from the couch. They're dry and easy to collect. No damage done to the couch that I can see.

I check my phone and see a new text.

Chuck Norris can hot wire any vehicle he gets into simply by putting his hands on the steering wheel and saying "vroom, vroom."

I smile until I remember that I'm pissed at Maya. Our usual Chuck Norris volleys won't make things right. She must be in Peoria by now, gearing up for the mission. Tarren's probably with her too, and they're all serious, cleaning their guns, strategizing how to find the angels, doing other blatant montage stuff while snow swirls against the window panes.

I put the phone away without responding and then power

up my girl, Starbuck. What I really need to do today is make us some money. The situation's pretty dire. Both Maya and Tarren think most of our money comes from the dating websites I put up. That's because this is what I told them. The websites do bring in some dough, but not enough.

The real way I make most of our money is playing poker online. I'm pretty sure Tarren would have a whole litter of cows if he knew how much of our money I put up, but I was pretty decent at it before. Ever since the coma though, I suck balls at Texas Hold 'Em. I couldn't bluff my way past a remedial kindergarten class.

This basically makes me a loser of epic proportions. It's my job to keep the family cashed, and I can't even do that. I'm thinking I'm going to have to resort to stealing some credit card numbers. I hate stealing from innocent people, messing with their lives, though I know, in the end, the banks will pay for it.

Stealing credit cards is ridiculously easy. I don't actually do the stealing. I just know the right dark net sites to swing by. Two years ago I made contact with a group out of Estonia that vacuums up truck-fulls of numbers through email phishing scams. They'll sell me ten numbers for 50 bucks. Five Hamiltons in exchange for a person's entire financial reputation. Sometimes I wonder if we're fighting the right bad guys.

I decide to hold off on going the criminal route and try to make it a good poker day instead. Only so long a losing streak can last, right? Screw angels and saving the world. We've got to eat. I dig into my duffle bag and take out my Starbuck action figure for inspiration. She was fond of the cards too, and with her bad ass spirit shining over me, I feel my luck changing already.

***

$16.34. That's how much I come out ahead after wasting four hours of my life, playing with a $2,000 bank. Hmmm, let's see that's about $4.00 an hour. I would've been better off slapping on some pimples and braces and begging a job out of McDonald's.

Real smooth, Gabe. Real bread winning going on. I take a deep breath and wish I'd brought some joints as I muck through the dark web and find my Estonians. I get a good deal on a dozen credit card numbers. Sorry good people who live honest lives and probably have a nice house, kids that went to college, and a yippy little dog in the back yard. Saving the world isn't always a pretty or honest business. Actually, it's just plain dirty most of the time. I remind myself that the banks always cover the fraud in the end. I don't mind giving those suits a little financial wedgie here and there.

When I get the numbers, the first thing I do is call up a little post office in some forgotten town between here and Fairwell and buy a PO box. Next, I dial up my favorite anarchist gun dealer. Franklin answers with an annoyed grunt but turns real agreeable when he hears my voice. I've been a good customer ever since I met him at a gun show about five years back. Franklin isn't one for government oversight, and his paranoia is my gain.

I order Maya and Tarren a new set of Glocks. Glock 19 for Maya's smaller hands. Tarren gets his preferred Glock 32C. I've also been thinking about getting us a third sniper rifle so we don't have to play musical chairs with the two we've got. Franklin and I discuss it, which takes for freakin' ever on account of his stutter. I know he hates it when I finish the word he's trying to pronounce, so I just let him go at it.

"What you n-n-n-need is a Bushmaster Carbon 15," he grumbles. "So, I've, so, so, already, so, got one in stock."

"Nah, I want another Barrett," I answer him. "Already know how to use it. You got an MRAD by any chance?" Oh, just thinking of that baby makes me want to drool.

Over the course of our convo, Franklin turns me toward the Bushmaster. Its highest selling point is that Franklin can ship it today and he has plenty of ammo. I bargain hard. That stutter isn't winning any sympathy points with me.

As we duel on the price tag, Franklin's cat starts meowing in the background. It's funny as hell to imagine the torn up old biker with a beard as long and gray as Gandalf's and a faded Hells Angels shirt barely covering his beer gut, petting a fluffy white cat on his lap.

Then again... I look at Sir Hopsalot on my lap. Nope. Totally different. Bunnies are cool as bowties.

In the end, Franklin throws in the red dot optic, the case, and two extra boxes of ammo for the rifle as part of the deal. Then we go head to head on ammo for the handguns. Tarren likes to shoot every day that he's home. I doubt he knows how fracking expensive those bullets are.

Right about the point I'm saying, "I want everything clean. Understand? Nothing hot. If I have to file off the serial numbers again myself we're going to have a problem," Amanda walks in. I give her a little wave. "Overnight it," I tell Franklin. I give him the PO box number and hang up.

"Thanks for breakfast and my kiss," I tell Mandy as I tuck my phone into my pocket.

Amanda smiles. Two bulging grocery bags hang off her

arms, and I take them both out of her hands. Feels like she filled them with bowling balls, but I don't let on one bit. Up on the counter they go, and I try not to wheeze like a little girl.

While she's cooking, kicking off her heels, and telling me about her day, I massage her shoulders. Actually, my stomach is starting to come back online, and I'm more interested in snatching some chips from the bag she's opened, but she leans her head back and groans, so I keep going with the massage, putting my thumbs into her neck.

Her hair is a tangle of orange curls. It feels so weird to me. Almost rough. Not like the way I imagine Francesca's hair would feel. God, I think about running my hands through those silky black waves.

"You're such an angel, Lee," Amanda says. "You really are."

I don't mean to, but my hands pause on her shoulders.

She looks back at me and mistakes the look on my face. "I wasn't meaning..." Her mouth gets all tight. "Lee, I know the way things are for us. I'm fine with it. I'm not pushing for anything more."

I get my hands going on her neck again.

"...unless you want to," she says in a small voice. For Mandy, this is a brave thing to say, and I recognize that. I kiss her shoulders and her neck.

"Mandy, I really like our time together. I like this. I like you. But with my job, I'm on the road all the time. It's a jungle out there."

"You could quit," she says.

"Nah, I've got to do it." I feel her shoulders tense beneath my fingers.

"Do you even like what you do?"

"It's important. I help people."

She places her hand over mine. "There's tons of virus protection software on the market. Most of it is cheap or free."

I lean in close, prop my chin on her shoulder. "Our software protects people...I mean their businesses, from a different kind of virus. Something most people don't know about. My company, we're the only ones who sell it. Without us, those viruses would hurt lots of businesses."

She steps away from me and starts mixing the veggies in one of the bubbling pots. "You sound like you're on a crusade."

Alright, time to squash this line of conversation. "It's not just that," I tell her. "The cancer. I'm in remission now, but the doc says it could come back any day. Fact is, it's pretty likely it will. I'm not looking to put that burden on anyone else. Wouldn't be fair." I can't help but think of Mom and that last terrible month of her life.

"Lee..." Mandy's got her head down, but I see a big tear rolling down her cheek. "I would take care of you."

This is when it finally hits my stupid brain that I've done her a real wrong. Taken this poor, lonely girl and given her a hope that just isn't there. I just never thought any girl would take the trouble of falling in love with me. What's the right thing to do here? I don't know. So, what I say is, "This is the way things have to be in order for there to be...uh, things. Okay?"

Mandy nods. "Okay." She wipes her tears away.

I drape my arms around her neck and kiss her cheek.

"Are you going to stay tomorrow?" she asks with a huffy breath.

"Yeah, sure."

"I took the day off."

"What do you want to do then?" The smell of the steak in the oven reminds me of how little I've eaten today, and I have to make an effort not to drool down the front of Mandy's blousy top.

"Whatever you want to do."

"Well, let's see..." I rock with her, and she's pulling herself together pretty well. "It's cold as hell outside, so..."

"Ice skating?"

I was thinking of something more bed-related, but I've never been ice skating before. This could be good too. "Sounds fun. Any place we can do that around here?"

"There's a rink just a few blocks away."

"Let's do it."

Her lips spread into a slow smile, so I back off and let her make dinner.

# *Chapter 7*

I'm better in the morning. The migraine has backed off enough that I can sort of pretend it's not there. I wake up when Amanda shakes me. My girl already has breakfast prepared. We eat it together in bed after I've thrown on some clothes. Nothing like the cold light of day for the self-esteem issues to kick in.

Mandy keeps insisting on helping me with the dishes, but I'm not having it. She cooked. I clean up and sing *Walking on Sunshine*. I tell her the only way she can help is by singing with me. After a good dose of over exaggerated begging on my part she actually does. Terrible voice, that one, which makes it all the better.

After dishes and a round of heavy petting, we're bundled up and on our way to this outdoor ice skating rink that Mandy says is only ten minutes away from the house. The place is nice. Smells like snow and looks like a picture you'd see on a postcard or on the wall of a nicer hotel than we usually book. The rink isn't too crowded, I guess because it's a school day, but a few people still go round and round. A girl with a shiny brown ponytail skates backwards like she was born on the ice, and some kids at the end push a hockey puck back and forth.

This is humanity. The good parts. The parts that Maya and Tarren are trying to protect up in Peoria. After a new Chuck Norris joke this morning, Maya texted about trudging through cold days and colder nights with nothing to show for it. I let her know I was still alive and almost sent her a Chuck Norris joke in return – I've got a hot one I've been saving up – but I just couldn't do it yet. Not after the hat.

I decide to kick Tarren and Maya out of my thoughts. Let them freeze their balls and lady parts off, respectively. I've got Mandy to keep me plenty warm. I lace up my skates hoping this won't be a disaster of the viral YouTube, *Tosh 2.0* variety. The whole gliding over ice on tiny metal blades thing would usually appeal to the stupid in me. I'd always been one for jumping right in and learning from scraped knees and ass landings. But now I feel anxiety creeping up. Wow, so I guess the coma turned me into a pussy.

Amanda already chided me about how my awesome duster wasn't warm enough on the ride over. As she sits down on the bench next to me with her rented skates in one hand, she produces an extra pair of mittens and a ridiculous purple knit cap from her coat. I'm not about to put that fugly thing on my head. Mandy gives me her worried eyes, like somehow this hat is an invincible shield against death by head cold. I put it on. This is karma justice for the stupid straw hat we always made Maya wear when her missing person case was all over the news last year. Tarren was dead serious about it, but I would harp on her because the damn hat just looked so stupid.

Mandy and I make our way to the ice. The skates are clunky and awkward, and my ankles struggle for balance. Then we're off the mats and, whoa...

We glide...kinda. I keep trying to walk, so we do this sort of clumping-gliding thing. And Mandy, damn, it's like I just threw a fish back in the water. She *swish swishes* next to me. We're arm-in-arm, but I'm the one clinging to her for dear life, not the other way around.

"You're good," I pant at her as two young boys rocket by us.

"I took lessons," she says, and a shy smile lights up on her face. "A long time ago. I know I don't look like it."

I wish she wouldn't do that, put down all her achievements.

We take a few slow laps, and Mandy coaches me. I don't usually go for someone telling me what to do, but in this case I need all the help I can get. Plus, Mandy's nowhere close to an automaton, know-it-all brother I could mention. God, if Tarren were a policeman, I bet every being on the planet would end up incarcerated for littering, not flossing twice a day, or failing to sneeze at the correct octave.

After a few more laps, I make myself let go of Mandy. No time like the present to grow a pair and ice skate like a man. A few laps later, I'm doing alright for myself, pushing against my skates, relaxing my body as I propel forward. I keep my arms a little out from my sides, and things get magical for a while. Here we are, Mandy practically soaring at my side, the two of us intermingling with all of these total strangers. I close my eyes and pretend, just for this minute of this hour of this day that I'm normal as fuck just like everyone around me.

Eye closing...ice skates...one of my lesser bad ideas, but still...bad idea. I cut one corner a little too hard. My skate lands wrong, and I go down. The pain is instant and deep, clawing up my hip and ankle. For a minute, I'm just on my ass panting, wondering where all the air went in my lungs.

Mandy is at my side asking worried questions.

I crack up laughing, and I'm more than a good enough liar to fool her into laughing with me while I take her hands and stand up. Fire dances inside my hip, and I feel yesterday's migraine still lingering in the back of my brain like a brewing storm cloud. I force myself to complete a few more tender-footed laps before I clump off to the bench. The skates are digging into my ankles anyway, but really it's because my legs feel like they got stuck in a tar pit.

Mandy makes to sit with me, but I can tell she wants to be on the ice, so I order her back out to the rink. She skates around for a few lackluster laps. When she comes back around, I stand up and stop her.

"Do what you want to do," I tell her. "All of these people are just background noise. Props. Plastic."

Mandy nods, her corkscrew curls bouncing. I put my gloved hand over hers.

"Show me what you got."

She laughs, but I see a glint in her eyes that I like. She finds a rounded corner of the rink out of the flow and spins on her skates. She even hikes her leg up like one of those fancy skaters on TV. I sit on the bench and watch. As Mandy spins and smiles and her orange curls whip around her pink cheeks, she really is beautiful.

The day goes by like water rushing out of a spilled cup. After ice skating we make it back to her place, and because we can't think of anything else to do, we build a snowman together. We have to pack the fine snow together hard to get it to stick. But it's one of those things where it's the journey, not the destination. The destination turns out to be a small, lumpish pile of snow with embedded pebble eyes, a carrot stick nose, and mismatched twig arms. Mandy loops a pink scarf around his no-neck but can't find a top hat. She names him Tyrion Lannister.

Afterwards, I take her out to dinner, because Mandy's probably bought out a whole grocery store feeding me these last two days. If my credit card was really as beefed up as I've implied, I would have ordered six entrees. As it is, I go with a cheaper pasta dish. Amanda just wants to order an itty bitty salad, insisting that she's on a diet, but I call BS all over that. She can go on a diet next week.

We laugh. We eat. I try to find out how many different ways I can make her blush and giggle (answer: a lot). The big dessert I order for us includes a brownie and ice cream and probably other stuff that would have tasted real good if I hadn't inhaled it. Mandy manages to get a few spoonfuls in and makes a happy little moan with each bite.

On the way back to her place, I feel the quicksand of exhaustion pulling me down.

"This has been, like, the funnest day of my whole life," I say to Mandy and rub her thigh when she stops at a light.

"Me too," she says. "It's so cold." She cranks the heat higher.

I hadn't even noticed. Actually I'm sweating. I know what that means. "I have to leave tomorrow," I tell her.

"Oh." She's looking down at my hand.

"Doctor's appointment."

"Of course."

"You got the green," I tell her just before some asshole honks behind us. With the heat rumbling in the vents and some girly music pulsing through the radio, I lower my eyes and that's it for me. I only barely remember taking zombie steps up the stairs and collapsing on her bed.

I wake up to her whispering something in my ear. "Lee? Lee?"

"Who's that?" I mumble.

"Amanda."

"I know," I say.

"What?"

My eyes are sinking shut. I couldn't prop them up with steel two-by-fours.

"Lee, I know you're tired. But can I...can I..." Her voice is a whisper, so far away.

"Yeah?"

"Touch you?"

"Sure baby. Do whatever you want." I'm about to fall asleep again, but the touch of her cold fingers jolts me back. She hesitates.

"Go ahead," I tell her, "S' okay."

She lays her hands on my lower back, under my t-shirt, then slides them up across my shoulder blades. That's the last thing I remember before going dark for the rest of the night. I have no idea what she did or how far she went, but I hope she got some pleasure out of my chicken bone body.

When I wake up the next morning, it's early. Too early. I'm shivering, and my bones ache like someone used them in croquet practice. Sick. Again.

Mandy is pressed against me, breathing slow and loud. I stroke her arm, studying all the golden hairs I'd never noticed before. Being close to someone. Feeling the heat of another body radiating onto mine. I want this. Every night. I want Francesca. To stroke her arm. To play with her hair while she sleeps. To make the bedroom our total world.

I get up quietly and take a cold shower to wash all the fever sweat off my body. I check my phone. Another Chuck Norris joke from Maya, this one sent at 1 AM. Jeez. They've really been keeping crazy hours.

`Make sure he sleeps`, I text her back.

I pack up my bag, put Sir Hopsalot in his cage, and, after searching through every cabinet in the kitchen, get the coffee going. It'd be easier for me to just walk out right now. Amanda would let me too. Wouldn't say a thing about it next time we got online together. But I know she doesn't deserve that kind of slinking exit. I set two mugs of steaming coffee on the nightstand, get back in bed, and lay a big wet kiss on her face. Then, right as she's starting to rouse, I tickle her.

Mandy screams and flails and ends up smacking me pretty hard in the ear.

"Gotta go pretty soon," I tell her, and this sobers her up. I pass her the coffee. She winces at the first sip, and I wonder if she's one of those crazies who dilutes their caffeine hit with cream and sugar.

"This was great though," I tell her, laying a kiss on her collar bone. "I forget how much I like being here. Being with you."

I think I said the wrong thing, because she stares at her coffee. Whatever she's thinking though, she doesn't say it. I put my things in the truck, and when I get back, she's standing in the kitchen in the beat-to-shit bunny slippers that I absolutely love. My fav is the left one with the missing eye, which I've named Nick Fury.

"Stay for breakfast?" she asks.

"I can't." Really. My joints are rusty, and my stomach isn't even close to appreciating the thought of solid food.

"But I'll stay for one more kiss. It's got to be a good one though." I almost add, "cause I have cancer," but decide at the last moment not to be a total ass. "Can you lay a good one on me?"

"Yes," she says, shy and sad again. Amanda walks up to me, brushes back her kinky orange hair, and gives me a long, lasting kiss with some tongue. Her breath is a little funky, but I make like she's the sexiest thing on the planet, pressing my body into hers, stroking her amazing breasts.

"Well, that'll certainly tide me over for the duration," I say as I pull back. I give her another quick kiss. "Bye, Mandy."

"Bye, Lee." She doesn't ask me when I'll be back. The girl's really more than I deserve, though I know she doesn't see it that way. I honestly think I do more good than harm, otherwise I wouldn't come at all.

She turns away so I can't see her face as I close the door.

## Chapter 8

The drive back home is about as pleasant as getting Force-choked by Darth Vader. My bones are a thousand years old, and apparently my brain has taken up percussion lessons in my head. An hour and a half later, Bubba and I cruise through Pueblo, CO, the last refuge of civilization before I plunge into the sprawling backwoods of my town, Farewell. I'm at a stoplight right next to the WalMart when my phone rings.

The hell?

Only three people on the planet have this number: Tarren, Maya, and Dr. Lee; and Maya's the only one who ever uses it, sending me her endless Chuck Norris texts and short mission updates.

She doesn't call. Ever.

Could be a wrong number or a telemarketer, but in my world it's more likely someone I love is bleeding...or worse. I pick up the call and nudge my way into the left turn lane, ignoring the honks as I swing Bubba into the WalMart parking lot. I'm pretty damn sure I don't want to be on the road for this conversation.

"Yeah?" I say. My fingers tap on the wheel.

"We have a situation." Tarren's voice is cold and empty. Someone's dead. Maya's dead. Or Maya's hurt someone, but she wouldn't...

"Could you be a little more fucking specific?" I say, and my voice is stupid loud.

Epic pause. "Maya has been taken."

I twist the wheel and screech to a halt, parked crooked across three spaces in the back of the lot. Tarren's words light a fire inside me. I look at my hand on the wheel, see the bones of my knuckles trying to push their way through my skin.

Angels are going to die for this. As many as it takes.

"So we'll get her back." My voice goes into hyper speed. "Tell me what we need. Guns, knives, scopes, whatever, and then I'll come out there and..."

"We need to initiate Styx," Tarren interrupts. Still that cold, robotic voice, like we're trading stock tips or discussing TPS reports. If I could punch his stupid face through the phone, I swear I'd do it.

"I'm coming and you're not stopping me." My voice is getting louder, trying to make up for all his bullshit calm.

"If she talks..."

"Maya won't talk!" I holler.

"If she does, then everyone is in danger, Lo, Dr. Lee..." Tarren pauses for just a heartbeat, "...and Francesca."

"Damn you," I choke.

"Get them out," Tarren says.

The phone is shaking against my face. "Don't you fucking leave her, Tarren. You find her, you bring her back."

We both know what I'm asking. Styx. I hate that word. Hate it so much I might just give my left nut to never hear it again.

ap—

Mom created Styx. I have to believe she did it out of love even though that word is like a nightmare, always stalking the very worst moments of my life. Styx is the code word we use when capture is imminent. It is a warning to the rest of the family to cut all lines of communication, abandon the house, get our allies out. It means we run and never look back so the angels can't find us no matter what information they pull from the captive.

Abandon one to save the rest.

Well, I don't do the abandon thing. Not ever. Better we all go down fighting and bleeding and cussing like sailors together than walk away from one of our own. I sure as hell won't let Tarren walk away either. He may act the cold-hearted hero on the outside – might have even been playing at it long enough to believe it – but I know the deepest parts of him are as squishy, human, and irrational as the rest of us.

"Tarren, promise me you won't leave her," I say into the phone. "Promise on Mom's grave."

A pause on the other end; one of those long, lingering Tarren pauses. "Don't go back to the house," he says finally. "Dispose of all the phones. Pick up a different vehicle…"

"I know how it works!" I'm screaming now, totally losing it. Maya's hurt. She's getting tortured, and I'm not there to save her, because she thought I was too weak. She and Tarren both, and they were probably right.

Tarren rattles off two email addresses he just set up so we can communicate without using our old phones, but I interrupt him again.

"Get her back!" I holler at the phone. "Get her…"

The dial tone hums on the other end. "No, no, no, SHIT!"

I pound the wheel with my fists, feeling the impact jar up my bones, but what does that matter when my sister is gone? *Just like Tammy.* I can't breathe. They have Maya. They'll hurt her. *Just like Tammy, just like Tammy.*

My brain is in full meltdown mode, but one thought finally gets me to stumble out of the truck and start stomping across the parking lot. I'm going to Peoria Fucking Illinois. Nothing's going to keep me here knitting a pair of socks for the soldiers overseas while Tarren plays the hero...assuming he doesn't turn tail with Mom's rule book up his ass. We're going to rescue Maya. There's just no other alternative that I'm willing to live with.

My strides turn into a jog. *I haven't been making Maya laugh.* This realization knees me in the balls. I've been so caught up in my own pathetic-fest that I haven't even been trying. It's my job to make sure she cracks that crooked smile and doesn't go sailing off into the sea of despair. I can't ever get Tarren back the way he was before Tammy died, but I can make Maya laugh. And I will. I swear I will.

I come up to the automatic doors, and damn, when did they start moving at the speed of glaciers? I get in, grab a basket, and manage not to punch out the dentures of the WalMart greeter who has the audacity to be pleasant and happy.

I head to the mobile phone department and drop a handful of cheapo, pay-as-you-go phones and some prepaid minute cards into my basket. I always carry an emergency $300 prepaid credit card in my wallet. This pretty damn well looks like an emergency to me. Next, I load up on snacks, piling protein bars into the basket and enough energy drinks to fuel the entire World of Warcraft community for a week. I hurry past the outdoor section on my way to the counter, stop, and backtrack. I go down the aisle, and my heart clobbers in my chest as I set eyes on a beautiful piece of equipment. I have just enough on the prepaid card to cover it. I tuck my prize under my arm and rush to the cash register like all of hell's fury was at my heels.

## *Chapter 9*

I connect my Bluetooth earpiece and give Lo a call as I peel out of the WalMart parking lot. My foot wants to go lead on the accelerator, but getting pulled over would just be one more bucket of shit in this shit hurricane. I force myself to stay right on top of the speed limit like I was just moseying my way to brunch after church.

Lo picks up on the third ring.

"What?" He somehow manages to pour his entire dickish attitude into that one word. Here's the thing about Lo – he's a full-on genius. A hair away from mad scientist if you ask me. Nothing wrong with having some smarts – Tarren's got IQ numbers in spades – but Lo has a way of always rubbing it in, letting me know that my mental crayon isn't only dull, but also broken and half melted in the sun.

Yeah, I know brains weren't one of the gifts God doled out to me, but I do my damned best to make up for it with roguish charm. Where's the appreciation for that? Roguish charm can get you out of a whole hell of a lot of situations, even some where too much thinking just gets in the way.

"It's me," I say.

He must know this is serious since I didn't open with an insult. "Tarren's dead," he says, and a waver hits his voice. Who knew the kid had feelings under all that goth crap he paints on his face?

"No."

A pause. "Maya." The heavy metal music crashing in the background disappears.

"We've been compromised," I say. "You and your mom need to get out. Head for the hills."

"Step-mom," he corrects automatically. "What happened?"

"Doesn't matter. Get out now." I'm doing my best Tarren impression, all half-uttered growls in a cold, *don't even think of messing with me right now* voice. "Don't come back, Lo. Seriously, you can't ever come back."

"Shit," he mutters. "How much time?

"None. Go."

"It's not that easy ass-wipe," he snaps back. "I've got things I'm working on. Important things. Samples. Experiments. I can't just sweep it all into a suitcase."

This is why Lo is such a little bastard. Here I am, trying to save his dweeby life, and he's bitching about it like I just pissed in his soup.

"Don't care. Move your ass, Lo!" I'm grinding my teeth, trying not to fishtail the slow-as-all-hell station wagon in front of me with the Disney Land family decal on the back.

"Was it Maya? Did she turn and join up with them?" Lo asks.

I whip around the station wagon and leave it and the speed limit in the dust. I dare a stupid cop to pull me over.

"I swear to God, Lo, you ever say something like that again

about Maya, and I'm going to kick you so hard in the balls, Mariah Carey will be jealous of the high notes you'll hit. Maya would never betray us."

I pass the sign to Farewell.

Before Lo can say anything that will further tempt me to hang up on this call and let the angels have a go at him, I list off the username and password for the second email Tarren gave me. "Soon as you get a new cell, email us the number. We'll go from there."

"Yeah? And then what happens? We stay in hiding the rest of our lives?" I hear a door opening on Lo's end. The scrape of something pulled from a shelf, followed by a small grunt. I hope that twiggy bastard drops a suitcase on his head.

I fly past the dwindling shops, and Bubba's wheels skid as I hit a gravel road without slowing. Snow covered pines and firs flash by like sleeping giants.

"And make sure you bring your mom, step-mom," I correct myself. It would be just like Lo to leave his feisty step-mom behind, let the angels descend upon her. Carmen's a little vacant in the head department, but she makes it up with lots of sauce and sass and so many curves that I bet she's a real rollercoaster in bed.

"She's my checkbook until I turn 18. She's not going anywhere," Lo says. He sounds a little out of breath. *Clinks* and *clunks* sound from his end of the call.

"Good." I'm about to hang up.

"Stay safe. Make sure Tarren does too," Lo says. There's that waver again.

Awkward. "Yeah, you too," I mumble and end the call before I do something crazy like start not hating the guy. I'm coming up on Dr. Lee's cabin anyway, and my attention immediately shifts to the occupants within.

I pull up into the driveway, turn off the truck, and take the spare Glock from the glove compartment. If they break Maya, if she talks, they could already have angels swarming us and our allies. The angel network is a far cry from the efficient machine it used to be when Grand's father ran things, but I've got a feeling our enemies would pull their broke-down clubhouse together for the chance to enact some hellacious revenge on us.

I wait inside the truck, listening to the wind blow through the trees around me. My eyes scan for any movement, any flash of color that could mean a coming attack. I try not to think about just how pathetic my aim was two days ago, or how exactly I could take on even a single angel when my video game life bar is 25% at best. We've always been the hunters. I take a second to appreciate how much I really, truly hate being on the prey end of the equation.

Everything is quiet. Pristine. Unnerves the hell out of me. I swing down from the truck and take careful steps up the icy porch steps. A small wreath of pine needles hangs on the front door, a tiny touch of green in this frozen forest of white. *Francesca*. My heart clobbers as I pound on the cabin door. I've just got to believe that Maya will hold out, that...

Francesca opens the door, her doe eyes wide and warm...still warm, even after everything.

"Gabe." She seems generally pleased to see me, though I don't know why. Her expression clouds as she gets a load of my face.

"I need to talk to Dr. Lee," I say quickly and add, "right

now," as if the urgency weren't plain enough.

"Okay." Francesca eyes the gun in my hand with unconcealed fear.

"Everything's fine," I lie to her. "We've just got...a situation." Damn, those were the same words Tarren used, and I'd wanted to punch him in the face for it.

"Do you want to come in?" Francesca is still the concerned hostess, even now.

"I need to stay out here. Get him now."

Francesca nods and turns, but Dr. Lee is behind her. His face is lined and leathery as a baseball glove. Same color too. Those dark eyes take me in.

"Tell me," he commands. The old man is sharp as broken glass. I almost expect him to read the entire story right off my face.

"Maya's been taken." No time to be all secretive in front of Francesca. "You need to get out, now."

"Don't you presume to kick me out of my house, Gabriel Fox," Dr. Lee spits back. "That girl was filled with rage and hurt. She was lost. And you only fed her with coals and vengeance. You led her down your own path. The path of ashes."

I hate when he goes into one of his drama-dripping rants. This is exactly where Tarren gets it from. When I was a kid, Dr. Lee's anger was scarier than the monster in my closet. His voice boomed like thunder and could shake all the lies and excuses out of me. Now, my eyes take in the peppered hair, the liver spots on his hands, the loose skin around his jowls. For as long as I've known him, he's been ancient, but he was never this old before – old enough to look weak and frail.

"Bellow all you want, but you're leaving." I realize that I

have to look down to meet his stony gaze.

"What is…" Francesca starts.

"If they come, they come," Dr. Lee says. "I'm not running anymore."

"And what about her?" I nod toward Francesca. "It's all fine and good to lay your weary ass down for a noble evisceration, but where does she go?"

"Please, stop," Francesca says, but I don't. I can't.

"How long until they find her? How long until they thank her for keeping me alive?"

Dr. Lee's lips press together so hard they look almost white. Finally, he says, "Francesca, we shall be taking a sojourn. You'll need to pack a bag."

Francesca looks at me, tears gathered in her eyes.

"I don't have time to explain what's going on," I tell her, "but it's not safe here. You have to leave."

"Who took Maya?" Her hand keeps clutching a long, dangling lock of black hair.

This is so not the time for the big reveal. "It doesn't matter…" I start.

"Has she been kidnapped?" Francesca's voice quavers.

We've asked way too much of her. Shown her flashes of something terrible without preparing her for the full-on nightmare.

I take her hands, though I know mine are cold and thin. "I need you to be strong for me right now," I tell her. It's the cheesiest of cheese, but that's what my idiot brain spits out. "I know I've got no right to ask that of you." I squeeze her hands. So warm. So soft. I want to kiss her fingertips. "Bring anything important that you can carry. You may not ever be able to come back."

She trembles, and for a second I think she might clock out of consciousness, but then she pulls her hands from mine and is in the house, rushing up the stairs. Good girl. My heart swells for her. That leaves me and Dr. Lee. My mother has already prepared him for the possibility, and I know, despite his squawking about going down with the ship, that he has a packed bag filled with plenty of money growing cobwebs in the back of his closet.

"Tarren's going to get her back," I tell him, and I really do believe it. Tarren can do things like this. I also want to tell him that he's right about Maya, how we betrayed her by stoking the flames of her vengeance, or however he put it, but we don't have time for that conversation.

As Dr. Lee retreats back into the cabin, I take up a position in the driveway and monitor the woods. All the hairs on the back of my neck are creeping up. Any moment a swarm of angels could descend upon us.

To their credit, Dr. Lee and Francesca are ready to go in fifteen minutes, though I swear the time went about as fast as a log rolling uphill. When we gather at Dr. Lee's old SUV, I hand over one of the clean phones I bought at Walmart and give them the info for our group email. I wish I had thought to steal a set of license plates in the Walmart parking lot to give to them. Too late now.

"Don't forget to eat," Dr. Lee tells me. "At least 3,500 calories a day. Lots of protein. And the vitamins."

"I've got it, Doc," I tell him and barely manage not to add, *now get in the car you stubborn bastard.*

Dr. Lee stands in front of me, looking a little ridiculous all bundled in his his thick black coat and furry hat with ear flaps. He reaches into his pocket and hands me several capped syringes. "You'll probably need these when you go to rescue her."

He didn't even have to ask if I was going to throw my skinny ass into the fray. "Adrenaline shots? I ask.

He gives me a look that says maybe my mental crayon is half melted in the sun after all. "B-12 injections. It'll give you a boost when you need it. But, Gabriel Fox..." For a moment, I'm a little boy again and he's about to tell me the injured baby raccoon I brought to him didn't survive the night. "...don't do anything stupid. If you can't get Maya back then you're all Tarren has left."

God, I wish he wouldn't talk like that. Like she's already gone. All I do is nod and help him ease into the passenger seat of their SUV. Francesca stands next to the driver's side door. When I come around to her, she gives me a hug. We don't have time for this, but my body betrays me, and my arms move, pulling her into me. That raven hair is on my cheek, soft as I imagined. Some tiny, crazy part of me imagines that if we could just stay like this and close our eyes, the entire world would just stop and leave us in peace.

I step back, my hands moving to her shoulders. She trembles. Because of me. Because of what we are. I've put her in danger.

"I'm sorry," I whisper.

"I'm afraid for you and for Tarren and Maya," she says back. "What is..."

"You have to go now." I pry my hands off her shoulders. I wish I had some brave, heroic words of comfort for her, but instead, I just watch as she swings into the driver's seat of the SUV. Dr. Lee meets my eyes. Disappointment galore in his stare.

*Be safe you stubborn old buzzard,* I think. It was the name Tammy always called him behind his back, but she spoke it with fondness. I wave them off and stay too long watching the SUV get smaller and smaller in the distance before it turns around the bend.

Now I should haul ass to Peoria Fucking Illinois to get Maya back, but...

I jump into my truck and rev the engine. Going home is dangerous, unnecessary, stupid...but the only pictures of my dad are on a shelf in Maya's bedroom. And then there's my lucky hat.

No way I'm going on the warpath without my lucky hat. I pat the chainsaw riding shotgun. There's more than one way to climb a tree.

# Chapter 10

Hat firmly in place, it's time to kick ass and take names. Bubba and I first stop over at a nowhere town about fifty miles away from Farewell. A McDonald's battles with Dairy Queen as the most prominent building in town. I suck in a big breath, clomp through the snowy parking lot of the post office, and gratefully receive the bulky packages addressed to my PO box. Franklin may not be a top notch conversationalist, but the stuttering gun dealer is solid on the follow-through. These guns and bullets will be put to good use.

Since I'm already here and pushing my luck, I might as well pick up a new ride while I'm at it. Bubba and I are thick as thieves, but he's got to stay behind. If all goes according to plan, I'll need something I can ditch in Peoria Fucking Illinois as soon as I meet up with Tarren.

I pull into an older looking apartment complex and scan the cars up for offer. I need something sturdy that can get me through a snowstorm in Peoria without drawing a lot of eyes. My gazes rests on a black Ford Escape. Yeah, escape is pretty much the name of the game here.

I troll the town, looking for a place to stash Bubba where

he won't be noticed or towed. Every minute seems to stack up on my shoulders. *They could be pulling out her fingernails or breaking her legs.* I have to get these thoughts out of my head. *They could be cutting her.* No convenient airport parking garages present themselves, so I finally use an old trick that Tammy first concocted. It requires a quick trip to the gas station and more of my dwindling cash, but soon enough I pull Bubba over on the side of the town's main drag and prop my bare bones For Sale sign in the back window.

I swing out of the truck and make my way back to the apartment complex where my new ride awaits. I make a casual stroll through the parking lot, watching for anyone coming and going or peeking out of the windows. The brown, boxy complex seems abandoned in the middle of the day. Just a few lonely vehicles remain here. I can't help but think, *God, who would live here? Did they all lose a bet or something?*

I slip my lock pick kit from the inside pocket of my duster, which I sewed on myself, and sidle up to the Escape. I try the door just in case and find it unlocked. *I guess it's time to find out that the world ain't a good place,* I think to the trusting sap who owns this SUV. I might actually be doing them a favor by giving them this little reality check. I slip into the driver's seat, eyes scanning, scanning, scanning for trouble, and just as I'm about to take out the latch on the steering column for a fast and beautiful hotwire, I glance in the rearview mirror and see the pink flowered baby car seat all strapped in the back.

Shit.

Stealing someone's ride is a dick move no matter what, but stealing from someone with a baby is the dickiest of the dicks.

Next to the SUV sits an old, rusted VW Bug that might have

been blue at some point in its misspent youth. Faded stickers compete for room on the bumper, and a PETA decal fills up nearly the entire back window.

Shit.

As soon as the Bug whines to life under my deft hands, I drive back to Bubba and transfer my bags – furry sidekick, guns, tools, food, clothes – to the rust bucket's tiny trunk, shoving aside an ungodly amount of cotton tote bags to make room. As soon as I'm clear of the town, I give Tarren's cell phone a ring, only to hit an immediate message that the number is no longer available. The stupid bastard must have trashed his phone already. I use my old phone to check the first email account Tarren created. No saved messages waiting for me. Of course. I hastily type out an email -- Where R U? On my way. Send addy or coords – and save the message to the unsent box. I check the second email account, the one I gave to Lo and Dr. Lee and save a message with the number of my new burner.

I can't help but crack a smile at our clear dysfunction. Mom would be shaking her head in horror if she could see us now. I can almost hear her voice, *Good planning saves lives!* Tarren lapped up that Kool-Aid. Maybe my head just isn't screwed on right, but I appreciate a little fluidity in a plan...except now when Tarren's gone underground, and I have no way of reaching him.

I know he's doing the radio silence thing on purpose, to keep me out of danger. Joke's on him. I'm dumb enough to go careening right into disaster all on my own if that's what it takes to save my sister. I give the Bug some gas, and with a little grumbling, off we go toward a blizzard and God knows what else.

***

My heart may be in it to win it, but my body is not on board with heroically returning to battle. On the way to Peoria Fucking Illinois, I plunge the first B12 syringe into my upper arm right after I cross over into Kansas. While I wait for that to kick in, I try all the tricks in the book to keep myself awake. I guzzle down a can of Red Bull as I switch past the NPR crap that comes on when I hit the radio button, find some heavy rock station, and turn it up hot and hard. The music throbs through my tender head, but it's all the better. I keep the window cracked, so the icy breeze hits me full in the face.

Over the hours, the world flies by, little nothing towns followed by long stretches of mostly empty road. I've been hunting angels since I was twelve and have seen just about every speck of dirt this country has to offer, except for Alaska and Hawaii, which, you know, don't really count anyway. The thing is, you turn on a TV anywhere, and you'll see all the buzz, glamor, and human mosh pits that are New York, Los Angeles, Chicago, Miami, yadda, yadda, yadda. But America, the real America is this right here, all these podunk water stops and vast stretches of farm land, deserts, mountains, and open solitude.

In the winter, the landscape is so colorless and cold that it makes your eyes want to turn inside out and see if anything interesting is going on in the brain. I hate that. Thinking doesn't ever lead me to good places. Once someone you love dies, all your mind ever wants to do is find that person again and comb over all the worst things you said to them. I have so many memories of Mom and of Tammy that want to come out. Especially those fights with Tammy where her eyes would almost go black with rage. Sometimes her ghost drags me by the ear into the past as if she were afraid of me forgetting her. But I won't. I can't.

And now with Maya taken...Jesus, the last place I want to be is inside my head right now. Dr. Lee's words sit on my chest like a 300-pound barbell. *Path of ashes*, he'd said. I tried, dammit! I tried to keep Maya away from the mission, but life has a way of trucking over you, leaving your guts all squished on the road no matter what you want.

With all the music blaring, I don't hear the text ping through, but I feel the vibration against my chest. I pull over right away, my rusted bucket whining as we skid onto the side of the highway. I barely miss hitting a sign for an upcoming gas station. Only Lo, Dr. Lee, and Francesca have my new number, which means someone is in trouble. I pull out my burner, hands shaky with the doom and gloom about to rain down. The screen is blank. No voicemail, no text.

I reach back inside my pocket and am surprised when my fingers wrap around a second phone. Shhhhit. My original is still on – the one I was most definitely supposed to get rid of the moment I sent my new number to all of our allies. If ghosts were real, Tammy would be slapping me on the back of the head right now, and Mom, well, Mom would probably be giving me one of those icy glares that Tarren has perfected.

I take the phone out and stare at it, wondering. Could Tarren be trying to contact me, letting me know that he swooped in and heroically saved Maya?

I swipe to unlock the screen, tap in my password, and find a text from Maya's number.

`I need to see you.`

I cradle the phone in my hand, chewing on the side of my cheek while my brain fumbles around like a fly caught in a jar.

Maya would have given me a Chuck Norris joke if everything was fine. Also, she sure as hell wouldn't ask to see me knowing that I'm stuck on the bench in Farewell. Which means…

I stare at the message again. *Who*?

I think I already know.

The angels that captured her are trying to ferret out her accomplices. This is an opportunity. My stomach has somehow grown arms and is punching itself. Tarren would know what to do. In the ten seconds since the text came in, he'd probably have a gigantic mental whiteboard with a multi-level matrix plan and already be on his way to kick ass, take names, and save the bloody day in that order.

Deep breath. Tarren is a dick wad who doesn't answer email. Screw him and all his day savingness. I can handle this. The inside of my cheek is practically sushi at this point. I just put Hannibal, MO in my rearview mirror, which means I've got a little under three hours to go before I descend on Peoria Fucking Illinois, probably longer considering the weather. My thumbs are sloppy as I reply.

`Sure, but tracking targets on other`
`side of town. Meet at 8?`

That will give me four hours to get there and…think of something.

I pull back onto the highway, and my eyes keep dashing down to the phone screen. Six eternal minutes later, the next text pings through.

`K`, it says followed by an address to some kind of park and instructions on where to meet.

B there, I quickly text back.

Hells yes I'll be there. I sit back against the seat, watching my breath plume in front of me. I've still got the window cracked, though I don't even need it now. I'm wide awake. Without Tarren I'll have to walk straight into this ambush alone. That's a ridiculously stupid move, even by my standards.

I grin as I gun the engine.

# *Chapter 11*

The Bug's headlights land on a whole bunch of blaring red taillights as I hit the dregs of the storm about an hour outside of Peoria. Huge snow drifts hug each side of the road as if this little ribbon of life had to be chiseled out of the ice. A half hour closer, and my wheels crackle over road salt. Snow flurries hit my windshield like fists. I have to put the wipers on just to keep things visible.

Traffic crawls. I resist the urge to get out of the car, throw my shoulder into the nearest bumper, and push those mothers a little faster. Wrecks line the side of the road, and the Bug's wheels don't take a liking to this slick pavement. We slip and slide, and it doesn't help anything that I'm jacked on adrenaline and exhausted at the same time.

My headlights glint off a snow topped sign. I think it's supposed to say **Welcome to Peoria,** but only the last line is visible – **Peoria** – like a statement. You are in Peoria now you stupid bastard. Deal with it.

I inch past the sign to try and get my first look of the town. The buildings and vast sweeps of flat land are so covered in snow that I can't tell a thing about it. I'm sure it's a nice enough town six inches down.

 Just for kicks, I check the shared email account. No messages from my brother. I try his phone again and listen to the pleasant voice of the operator tell me that the number I have dialed is no longer in service and I should just go enjoy a nice healthy glass of paint thinner. Might have made up that last part.

 I don't like this. One isn't just the loneliest number you'll ever do. It's also the most vulnerable number. One gets stabbed in the back. One gets ambushed. One gets introduced to the wrong side of unfriendly fists.

 "Not alone, though, right?" I murmur to Sir Hopsalot who sits patiently in his carrying case. "There's an extra carrot in it for you if we survive this thing."

 After swinging into Starbucks for a bathroom break and the biggest cup of plain hot coffee they make, I head on over to our designated meeting spot an hour early. My joints howl, and my eyelids feel like paperweights. As soon as I nudge the Bug into a parking spot, I chug the coffee and jab another B12 syringe into my arm. Dr. Lee told me to wait 24 hours between injections, but if I'm not alert right now the game is up.

 Alright, time to stop bitching and start assessing the scene and stuff. I try to be all serious about it like Tarren would, furrowing my brow as I look around. I'm at some kind of Rec center. In the poorly lit parking lot, a few American trucks and SUVs sit in the spaces. To my right, a wide, snow-covered field might hide baseball diamonds or soccer fields. According to the instructions texted by the angels, I'm supposed to cross the fields and wait at a small playground on the other end. I squint into the night, trying to see the playground, but the large field lights are off, and darkness swallows the landscape just a few feet in. Wow, creepy much? I'm pretty sure I'd rather eat an entire spoonful of my own toe fungus than set one foot into that death arena.

I huddle in the Bug, slurp the dregs of my coffee, and decide on a plan. It's a good one: figure out who the angel is, shoot him a couple of times in non-lethal places as soon as he turns his back to walk into the field, and use every nerve pinch I know until he tells me where my sister is.

There. Done. Gabe's recipe for instant family rescue.

Franklin was kind enough to throw in a good-customer silencer in his weapons delivery, and I screw it on now to the barrel of my Beretta. They don't actually silence a gunshot – none of that dainty spitting you hear on television – but do dampen the loud crack of gunfire. That'll be useful if I end up in a shootout in the parking lot.

I watch an SUV pull up. My fingers tighten on my gun, and I roll down the window just a little using the ancient hand crank. Two bundled up kids tumble from the back of the SUV and start slipping and sliding toward the entrance. A weary mother follows, holding a thick parka closed around her body and two small hockey sticks under her arm. My hand relaxes, and I crank the window back up to keep out the cold. As soon as anyone walks toward the snow logged fields, I'll know my angel.

As I wait, I think back to my last target practice...and then I stop thinking about that. Instead, I play every game Tammy and I ever made up to help keep each other awake on long stakeouts, including such classics as *Would you do it for $25? Which pinch hurt more? How many animal noises can we make before Mom/Tarren tells us to shut up?* Half an hour later, a gray truck rumbles into the parking lot. I tuck myself further down into the front seat, keeping just my eyes above the window. The truck slides into a space in the back corner of the lot, close as possible to the fields. *Bingo, Yahtzee, and Connect Four.*

I tighten the grip on my gun and slip out the door, away from their view.

*Please don't let any civvies come into the parking lot right now,* I pray. One set of eyes from an innocent bystander, and I'm going to have a huge problem. It's worth the risk though – Maya's worth the risk.

After a whole frickin minute, both doors to the truck open, and two figures drop out.

Two. Damn. Change of plans. I'll have to head shot the first and then proceed with my original plan on the second, assuming he doesn't have time to unleash some weird power like spewing jet streams of volcanic lava at me.

The two angels are wrapped in heavy jackets, and I can see the puffs of their breaths as they come together and murmur. I wait for them to start making their way across the snow covered field just to be sure. Once they start moving in that direction, I'll trail at a distance and hit them as soon as they're out of sight of the parking lot.

The two angels pull on plastic animal masks.

In that instant everything goes to shit. Total shit.

Not angels at all.

# Chapter 12

I watch the two guys slink off across the field, their flashlights turning the snow golden as they sink ankle deep with each step.

What....the...fuuuuccccckkkkk?

I'd know those dopey masks anywhere. I'm dealing with the douches from the video I took down. *But...but...*my mind sputters. How the hell did they get Maya's phone? Are they the ones who grabbed her?

No way. It'd be like losing a fight to a Smurf. Maya is trained. She's got angel speed and reflexes. These guys...they look like they read too many comic books and raided a zoo gift shop.

I let the reality of the situation sink in. *Ohhhh, ho, ho,* when I rescue the shit out of Maya, she and I are having a serious conversation about getting abducted by proper bad guys.

And now I'm stuck. The humans have gone off to set up their grand ambush of me, and it's not exactly like I can go tromping out there and shoot them in the face. Not only are humans off limits in general, but these bumbling idiots are actually on our side. Maybe I could talk to them...except the fields are too empty. Nowhere to hide. I might as well wear a huge target on my ass if I took one step out of the parking lot. Which means I wait and think of a new plan.

My phone purrs in my pocket.

*Oh thank Captain Picard's glorious bald head.* Tarren is finally getting with the program. I could so use his scowly self right now.

"Bout damn time," I say into the phone.

"Hello?" The reedy voice on the other end is uncertain.

Don't tell me Tarren got his ass kidnapped by a malicious AV club.

"Who is this? I don't have time for games," I snap into the phone.

"Uh...dude, I'm just calling about the truck."

Truck?

"The one for sale on Taylor Street," the guy clarifies. *Holy Special Olympics, Batman!* Did I seriously write my real phone number down on the sign? Worst. Vigilante. Ever. I think the spirit of James Bond just hung himself in despair.

"Yeah, yeah, course," I say as I tuck myself back into the Bug and close the door. No reason to freeze my dick off outside.

"How much..."

"Twenty grand."

"What? No way."

"That's a steal for a talking truck," I assure him.

"A...."

"Yeah, she talks. You know, all Magnum P.I."

"Uh..."

"You're probably wondering why I want to sell. Thing is, we've just grown apart these last few months. We used to be best friends, singing songs together as we drove the highways, occasionally fighting crime, but then, well, probably shouldn't be telling you this, but full disclosure and all, I kind of..." I sigh dramatically, "I fell in love with her."

"Look, uh..."

"I know, it's crazy!" I cry. "You don't have to tell me. But the heart wants what the heart wants. I told Jennifer, that's her name. I got wasted one night, sat in the driver's seat, and just poured my heart out while I stroked her steering wheel. Told her I wanted to take our relationship to the next level, but she just..." I let my voice waver. "She just didn't feel comfortable with that. And so what am I going to do, man? When I put my hand on her stick now, I just...things are so awkward. Even a drive to the gas station is torture." I sniffle. "So we talked it over and...and we both agreed....Hello?"

The dial tone greets my ear. He actually held on longer than I would've guessed. I don't even know I'm shivering until I hear my teeth chattering against each other. Probably should have grabbed an actual coat from home while I was getting my lucky hat. I love this duster to death, but Mandy was right. It doesn't do anything against sub-zero temperatures. I turn on the engine, crank the heat, and start channel surfing the radio for some good figure-out-how-to-get-stubborn-human-dickheads-to-talk-without-shooting-them music. Every radio announcer seems to be talking non-stop about the storm and the growing body count. Apparently a cop died this morning. Heart attack they say.

Yeah, and I own a talking truck. Angels are here. Angels, us, and this new band of posers. What a combo. *Hmmmm.* Something starts to click in my brain. Did Zoo Friends think

Maya was an angel? Did they see her toss a car over her shoulder and then go after her? *And what did they do to her?* My heart does this weird squirming thing. If they're wannabe vigilantes, what's the chance that they abducted my sister instead of just putting a bullet through her head?

*Maybe they needed information,* I tell myself, but it's a long shot. We don't keep angels alive for questioning – never have. It was Mom's number one rule. We take them out, W*ham, Bam, Thank you, Ma'am*. What if these guys are the same? What if they…. I press my forehead against the wheel, wishing my brain would just shut off, that I didn't feel sweaty and freezing at the same time.

I assume the Zoo Pals will man the ambush for at least two hours, but an hour later I see them trudging back, masks shoved up, noses red. Sad, sad, sad. Tarren and I would have staked the holy hell out of that playground. We would have been there all night, taping our fingers back on when they froze off.

I watch the guys come closer. The tall, pale one with the penguin mask resting on his forehead hunches over, hands plunged into the pockets of his parka. The shorter, Asian guy next to him looks pissed.

Lucky for them, I'm going to get their spirits up. I move into position, leaning casually against their Chevy truck. The wetness of the snow seeps into my jeans, and I shiver. My legs feel weak, but I keep a bored expression on my face.

Penguin seems to grow taller as he approaches. He might even have an inch or two on Tarren but only half the muscle mass. An ugly red welt stands out on the side of his head. The Asian guy looks young, maybe not even out of his teens yet. His long face is twisted into a snarl. His Tiger mask reminds me that he was my favorite in that pathetic video that they made. He'd bungled the script, shouting about how he was going to kill all the angels they found.

I smile at the memory, but God help them if they've hurt my sister.

They spot me and their steps slow. The tall one looks confused, and the short one just gets angrier.

"Oh, I get it," I call out to them. "The masks are like some kind of living artistic statement. Something about the animal trapped within. Very deep."

The tall one frowns and stops. They haven't put two and two together, and I don't blame them. They came here looking for a roided out angel. I don't exactly fit the bill.

"That's our truck," the tall one says. He moves to do something – maybe just open the driver's side door, maybe try to shove me back. I take one swift step toward him, grab his arm, and throw my shoulder into his sternum. The beauty of this little trick is that I use his own momentum to flip him over my shoulder. He lands hard, the breeze whooshing out of his lungs.

"Guess they don't teach you that in art class," I say.

Tiger has smartly reassessed the situation. He steps back and quickly struggles out of his big jacket. When he moves into a basic defense pose I'm almost glad for it. This shouldn't be so easy. A large chain hangs around his waist like some kind of retro belt.

"Heavy pants, huh?" I say.

"You wanna fight, asshole?" he spits out in this deep, low voice that's all show. "Try me out."

"Okey-dokey." This is going to be fun. Sure, I may be at the end of my strength, and maybe every bone in my body aches with fever, but I've been training in martial arts my entire life – judo, karate, tai chi, krav magna, MMA. You name it, and I've practically imprinted it on my DNA. And, unlike the majority of chain-belt-wearing ass hats I might mention, I don't spend two nights a week sparring at a dojo in the local strip mall. I get plenty of real world practice against guys who are a hellauve lot faster and stronger than me.

Tiger wants to take the first punch, so I let him have it. He edges closer and tries to go high with an elbow strike. He's terrible about broadcasting his moves and not nearly as fast as he thinks.

Not fast like me.

I twist away from the incoming blow, spin behind him, and give him a little push to get him off balance. He stumbles forward, and I laugh. He's so pissed, I expect to see steam coming out of his ears. He grits his teeth and comes at me again. This time he feints a round house but drops low to try and sweep my feet from under me. I duck the arm, grab his leg, and pull. He goes down on his back and rolls. Not a terrible recovery. He might be salvageable.

Just as Tiger makes it to his hands and knees, I give him a knee to the ribs – not that hard, but it doesn't take much. He goes down with a grunt.

"Stay," I tell him and try really hard not to grin so much. Probably not great for his ego.

I turn to Penguin, who's managed to pull himself into a sitting position against the tire. He wheezes like an 80-year-old pack-a-day smoker. Something tells me that he's my best bet for information. Just as I open my mouth to start my first round of questioning, I hear Tiger's feet scramble against the ground behind me, the warning *clink* of his chain. I wait, allowing him to ready his attack. Just as he takes his first step, I turn, duck the wild swing, and give him an upper cut to the jaw. My knuckles explode with pain, but he staggers back and blood spurts out of his mouth. I strike again, a swift punch across his face. My knuckles are begging for mercy, but Chainy goes down with a gushing nose.

"Stay," I tell him again and shake out my hand.

Bird Brain watches me cautiously. I reach inside my duster and pull out the Berretta with silencer affixed. Smart of me to cut those holes in the pockets of my jacket to accommodate the silencer. The guy's eyes widen for a moment, but then he takes a long, slow breath and meets my gaze.

Color me a tiny bit impressed.

"I don't like that one," I say motioning to Chainy, who tries to catch the blood waterfall in his hands. "He called me an asshole. Point of fact, I'm actually a pretty nice guy when you get to know me."

Bird Brain's face is pale. "Are you one of...of...them. An angel?" His voice is soft but steady. I keep both guys in my line of sight and the gun tucked in front of my body, shielding it from view of the other cars in the parking lot. I'm pressing my luck, and I know it. Every second I stay out here is another second someone could walk out of the Rec center or pull into the parking lot.

"I've got the talking stick," I tell Penguin and give my gun a little wave. "So, I'm going to ask you a question. You're going to answer me, or you'll be shelling out for a pine box for your fashion disaster friend over there, capiche?"

Bird Brain nods slowly. Chainy looks like he wants to take another run at me. "Don't even think about it," I tell him and try to put menace in my voice. Hard to play the badass when my teeth are audibly chattering, but I do my best. "I've got a real itchy trigger finger. You even fart over there, and it might be the last thing you ever do."

Chainy eases back down, but he doesn't look scared. Not good. You find a man who isn't afraid to die, and you've got one dangerous motherfucker on your hands. Luckily, Bird Brain looks scared enough for the both of them.

"You texted me on a phone that belongs to my sister," I tell Bird Brain. "I'm rather fond of my sister. The first thing you're going to tell me is whether she's alive. The second thing you're going to tell me is where she is."

Bird Brains stares.

"Start talking," I bark. *Lame, lame, lame,* but my heart is jackhammering waiting for his answer. *Please, please, for every drop of blood in my body, let her be...*

"She...she's alive," the guy stutters.

I let out the breath I didn't know I was holding. I couldn't dip those words in gold to make them any more precious.

"But....she...." Bird Brain winces, "...she escaped."

# Chapter 13

My new friends introduce themselves as Penguin and Chain, and the three of us take a little walk across the parking lot, my gun keeping things pleasant as can be. I invite my captives to take the front seats of the Bug, while I slide in back. As soon as the doors close, I immediately feel less conspicuous, and it's a hell of a lot warmer in here too. I keep my Berretta tucked in close to my side and trained on the dumbass with the chain belt.

I order Chainy to hand me Sir Hopsalot's carrying case, and once I place it securely next to me on the seat, we're ready to begin. Bird Brain and I do a bit of conversating about my sister. Apparently Zoo Pals was on the trail of a different angel. They crossed paths with Maya and decided to abduct her instead. When he mentions cuffing her to a chair for interrogation, my trigger finger gets itchy.

"Skip ahead," I growl for their own safety.

Whatever Bird Brain hears in my voice makes him swallow and stutter on his next words. They cut Maya's questioning short when one of their team members – Bear or Beard or Burt, whatever – got a hit on another angel. I immediately have a million and one questions about their angel detection system, but I stay on track with Maya. I'm proud when Bird Brain glumly explains that Maya pulled off an impressive-sounding escape, bagging the angel the team brought back in the process and basically saving the lives of all of these jokers. Not that they're willing to admit it.

"Okay, she coffins the wings, and then what does she do?" I say, mostly to myself. Answer: Find Tarren, except my brother has apparently checked into the Fortress of Solitude and is completely unreachable.

The peanut gallery pipes up. "Bear doesn't think she killed the other a...angel," Bird Brain says, like his mouth has a hard time pronouncing the word "angel."

"Course she killed him," I snort at him. "Only a slobbering lummox keeps angels alive and tries to question them."

Chainy mutters something under his breath.

"What?" I snap at him.

He sighs as if this were the most pointless conversation in the world, like he wants to talk opera but we're just sitting here trading dick jokes instead.

"She didn't kill him," he says.

"Look, I know my own damn sister and..."

"Bear's cameras have caught at least four of those soul sucking monsters around the city in the last two days. There's a big group of them here dropping people like flies. He told your sister, or whoever she is, about it, told her to find the nest and take it out. She tranqed our captive; didn't kill him. Finch saw the whole thing go down."

"She's not that stupid," I tell him, but a knot is twisting in my stomach. None of it even makes sense. How could the Bad

News Bears here have tripped over four sets of wings in the same town? The only time we've come across a group of wings that big was in Poughkeepsie. The magnitude of this shitstorm begins to rain all over me. Those four angels could only be the tip of the iceberg, or, for a better comparison, only the cockroaches who didn't scurry fast enough out of the light. Would Maya risk keeping the angel alive to try and discover their home base?

I know what Tarren would do. *He'd run right into the fire and take as many of them down with him as possible. Probably look totally awesome doing it too until he bled out and they put his head on a pike, all Ned Stark style.*

The knot in my stomach tightens. If I can't get in contact with Tarren, then Maya can't either. She's out there alone. *What next, Maya? How far would you go?*

The fact that I can't answer these questions makes me want to retch all over the worn vinyl of this Pinto wannabe. I notice that both guys are turned in their seats, looking back at me. Great. Have we just been sitting in silence while I realize I hardly know my own sister anymore?

"So, who the hell are you guys anyway?" I manage.

"We're the Totem," Bird Brain answers right away.

I remember the name from their so-horrible-it's-actually-good video. I should probably do the right thing and stifle my laughter. I don't do the right thing.

The Asian kid's face bunches up with anger. "These monsters, they're just killing people, and no one's doing anything about it!"

"There are people doing something," I correct him. "And you're getting in our way."

"Are you human?" Bird Brain cuts off whatever Chainy was going to throw out. His big brown eyes are serious, and somehow that cuts through my panic giggles.

"Through and through." I hold up my left hand and show them my palm. No angel seams of doom Xing through my skin.

"But your....sister...." He seems to have trouble with that word.

"It wasn't her fault," I tell him. "She was changed against her will." Guilt slugs me in the gut as I remember that night. If only I'd kept a closer tail on Maya. I'd thought the campus was safe, that Grand would never be so bold.

"She said..." These words seem to be costing Bird Brain something big. "...Buffy said she was on our side, that she didn't kill anyone in...." his hands grip his knees, "...in Marymoor Park."

Buffy, huh? Nice. Maya either used the nickname I gave her as a cover, or they took it from her fake license. I remember her face when I handed that baby over to her. Man, if looks could lop off testicles, I'd be singing soprano in the choir. Another thought nags at me. Marymoor Park sounds familiar. I chew on it a second, and then it comes to me.

"Yeah, that was Redmond, Washington. What, about half a year ago?"

The guy's neck goes red. "Five months."

It's coming back to me in fits and starts. Harold Krugal. All those dark, slimy memories. I'd had to hurt him. Not my best moment, but it led us to his network of angels...to Poughkeepsie.

"People were going tits up in the park," I remember out loud. "I'll never forget that mission. Turns out the angel was this little girl, fifteen years old I think, doing all the murdering. Couldn't help it really. The hunger does that to them, all the full angels. M—Buffy is different."

Weird that Maya mentioned Marymoor to Bird Brain. I don't see the connection. She's been on a dozen missions since then. Why spill the beans about that one?

"Different?" the guy mumbles, and his face is scrunched up like the universe shoved a spoonful of anchovies into his mouth.

"Yeah, Buff, that's her nickname, is only half an angel, a hybrid. She doesn't kill people. Just rats. You knew that, right? She must have told you."

The guy's face is stricken, making the red, angry welt on the side of his head stand out even more. I'm kind of worried that he might actually blow a heart valve in a second here.

"But she's…I saw…." the guy stammers. Something is going on inside his head, but I don't have the time to play therapist. My energy reserves are gone, and I've got no place to go. Tarren is in the wind, Peoria Fucking Illinois is apparently a snake pit of angels, and Maya might be trying to play snake charmer all on her own.

Wow, so we're much more fucked than usual.

Then I have a wonderful, big-ass light bulb moment. "You said you took a phone off this other angel you brought in?"

Bird Brain nods.

"Then we can find them," I say with more confidence than I feel.

The two guys upfront are silent.

"Let's go get it," I tell them impatiently. When they both look back at me uncertainly, I realize that I have to spell it out for them.

"We're teaming up you numbskulls. You need my help more than you can possibly know." I don't mention the fact that I'm practically dead on my feet.

"We don't need anything from you," Chainy snarls. Something about him has been nagging at me besides just his delightful personality. His face looks familiar, but I can't place it. Maybe he was in some herpes commercial or something.

"You really hunt them? You know how to do it?" Bird Brain's voice is soft, a little awed. He's definitely the only one in this pair worth talking to.

"I've been putting those assholes in the ground my whole life," I tell him, "and I'm still breathing." *Barely*. "You need me or your little totem pole is going up in flames." *Nice!*

As a gesture of goodwill, I switch the safety on and slip my Berretta back into the inner pocket of my duster.

"We should take him to Bear," Bird Brain says to Chainy.

"I don't trust him." Chainy touches his swollen, blood-crusted nose.

"He could have killed us, but he didn't. You heard him, he knows how they work, how to kill them."

I lean against the back seat and wait for the inevitable.

Chainy sulks. Bird Brain looks back at me, "Okay, we need to take you to Bear."

"Yeah, sure, can't wait to meet him. Mind if we pick up some food on the way?"

\*\*\*

Chainy goes ahead with the truck. Honestly, it's a relief to get his angry ass out of my sight. Kid like that might kill you in your sleep. Bird Brain tells me he's alright, but I know the difference between good crazy and bad crazy when I see it. I order Bird Brain to drive the Bug. Outwardly this seems like a good defensive move on my part, but really it's because my vision is starting to go swirly, and my hands are shaking like pennies on top of a churning washing machine.

I guide Bird Brain to the first pair of golden arches that I see. At the drive-thru speaker, I lean over him and order three burgers, two containers of fries, and the biggest drink size they have. When we get to the payment window, Bird Brain looks at me. I raise an eyebrow, and he pulls out his wallet. He goes for a credit card.

"Cash, you idiot." I roll my eyes for good measure. When he complies and we move up to the next window, I give him a look. "Tell me you haven't been using your credit card all around this town."

He grimaces.

"God almighty," I sigh. "Is your cell phone registered in your name?"

Silence.

"You been logging into any websites here using your real name?"

More silence.

"You seriously have no clue what you're doing, huh?"

He looks so shaken that I have to smile. Kid is growing on me. Maya was Queen of Disasters before Tarren and I – mostly me – whipped her into shape. If I don't help Bird Brain and his psycho friends cover their asses, then who will? In fact, I'm probably the one and only thing between them and utter bloody doom. *This is my good deed of the year,* I think up to God. *You'd better send me loads of good karma for this...please...amen,* I add.

A hot, probably under-age girl hands over the bulging bags of food. I give her a wink and get a little blush in return. Ahhhhhhhh, the smell of grease and meat and more grease. Cheap and delicious calorie overload is definitely one of the main reasons we have to save the world from an angel takeover.

"Drive," I say to Bird Brain and dig into the bag. He eyes me like maybe he's under the mistaken impression that I'm in the mood to share. I give him a look that says he's going to have to hijack his own superhero wannabe if he wants to earn a meal. I scarf loudly and probably let out a few groans too. Bird Brain doesn't do a good job of hiding his discomfort.

"So...not a vegetarian then," he says meekly.

I raise an eyebrow at him.

"I guess all the PETA stickers are a cover?"

It takes me a moment, and then I remember that this piece o' crap death bucket is slathered in "Animals Are People Too!" stickers.

I give Bird Brain a big smile. "That's adorable."

"What?"

I just keep grinning at him and watch his frazzled meter tick up and up and up. I do this to Maya all the time too. She hates it.

"What?" Bird Brain says again, louder.

"You think this is my car." I go back to eating, all nonchalant. He stares at the wires dangling from the steering column, and I can tell when it clicks in his head. He pretends, very poorly, not to be concerned, but I see him start glancing in the rearview mirror, probably looking for cops.

"We're almost there," he says. His voice is still a little high, but I appreciate the effort at playing cool. Too bad I have to totally mess with him for roughing up my sister.

"I assume you've been using diversionary driving tactics," I say as I dig deep into the fry container for the last few survivors.

"What?" Doubt creeps into his voice.

"In case we're being followed by the enemy," I answer as if this is the most obvious thing in the world. "There's a posse of angels running around, and you kidnapped one of them. They could be tracking you right now with their super senses. You did know that, right? About the super senses?" A fry falls in my lap, and I fish it out.

"Yeah...course," he lies. I watch his knuckles whiten on the steering wheel.

"Well, if you weren't using diversionary driving tactics, they could follow you right back to your hideout. They'll wait to take you unaware, probably while you're all sleeping. I've seen it before." I shake my head solemnly. "Messy, messy business. But if you've been using diversionary driving tactics, we're fine."

I sit back in my seat and lick the wonderful grease and salt off my fingers. We stop at a light. I turn my head.

"SHIT!" I scream, jerking up from the seat.

"What?" Bird Brain twists around in his seat.

"We've got company," I say, my voice grim. "Yep, definitely angels. A few cars back. Damn."

"Where?" Bird Brain yelps. He scans the cars.

"Act cool!" I shout at him, pulling the gun out of my coat but keeping it below the window. "Okay, put this baby in reverse. Soon as the light turns green, you perform a Gallifrey maneuver, get me in close..." I roll down the window as I speak. "I'll blow them both to hell, and then you've got to get us out of here. Got it?"

The kid is so white I think he might pass out. I can't help it. I crack up. The light turns green, and Bird Brain stares at me, unsure. The car behind us starts honking its ass off.

"Move, you idiot," I manage between gasps as I drop my gun back into my pocket.

Bird Brain has the sense to switch the car from reverse back into drive, and we sail forward. "You're...you're really messed up," he mutters.

I roll up my window, mercifully shutting out all that freezing air. "Comes with the territory. You wanna do what we do? Check your sanity at the door."

# Chapter 14

Bird Brain pulls us into a freakin' Marriot of all places. I try not to let the poshness of the place immediately piss me off. Marriot wouldn't even take a dump at the places we usually stay. As Bird Brain parks, I think, *It's better to buy bullets than a stupid mint on the pillow anyway.*

"How many in your crew?" I ask as we walk toward the entrance. Bird Brain plays pack mule, carrying my duffle and tool bags. I grip Sir Hopsalot's carrying case. Poor guy has been in the case all day. He's so good about it, but I know I'm a craptastic owner. Then again, he was originally supposed to be Maya's dinner, so it's all about perspective.

"Five...no, four," Bird Brain mumbles.

"You don't know how many people are on your crew?"

"We had five...this morning." Bird Brain looks away.

This is news. He didn't mention losing a member in his quick rehash of this afternoon's events. My stomach tightens.

"Who..." I begin nervously.

"Puma," Bird Brain answers.

"No, who killed him?" I clarify. I remember Puma now from the video the Totem posted. He was the cocky son of a bitch who couldn't give cardboard a run for its money in the acting department.

"The angel. Uh, the, not Buffy. The other one."

Wheeeewwww! Big exhale. Maya didn't fall off the no-killing-humans wagon. Not that those bastards didn't have it coming, putting her in cuffs.

"Sorry man," I say to Bird Brain as we make it to the front entrance. "Dangerous business. I can help you with getting rid of the body."

He gives me a probing look, not entirely sure I'm being serious.

The huge revolving front door of the hotel looks like a death trap to my blurring vision. I can almost hear a woman's proper British voice announcing in my brain, *Imminent bodily shutdown in...twenty minutes.*

I shadow Bird Brain's step exactly as he takes on the door, practically spooning him in the process.

"Uh...okay," he murmurs as we make it through into a huge, polished reception area.

I decide to pretend our little door mamba was completely ordinary. Actually, I forget all about it the second I raise my head and look around. Holy Churchill's spleen, this place makes every motel room we've ever been in look like a dumpster dive. Huge chandeliers hang from the ceiling, plush furniture dots the lobby, and a colorful abstract painting hangs behind the reception area. I don't see stale wads of chewing gum anywhere.

Classical music gently spills out of speakers, and people skitter around in controlled chaos. My sneakers squeak across the tiled floor as I move out of the way as two men in suits zoom by clutching the handles of small black roller cases. I also note the cameras and weave a drunkard's path around a few columns, keeping my face turned away. They'll catch glimpses of me, but not enough for an easy ID.

Bird Brain watches my little dance, skepticism written all over his face. Yeah, I burned him good with that little trick in the car. Probably not the best idea in hindsight, but still utterly worth it.

"Cameras," I grumble to him. He looks up, probably noticing them for the first time. I'd bet my left testicle that he and every member of his stupid Totem have been sauntering through the lobby in full, glorious view. *Great*. We've been together all of a half hour, and they're already compromising the shit out of me. I really should have thought this through better, but it's too late now. The cheerful British narrator inside my head announces, *Imminent bodily shutdown in...17 minutes*.

When we make it to the elevator, I keep the brim of my hat low and stare straight at the floor.

"Will your crew be more receptive than Chad?" I ask as Bird Brain hits a button for the 23rd floor.

"Chain? Yeah, Finch and Bear are cool."

The doors open with a stupid pleasant *ping*. "Lead the way."

We scuffle over nice carpet that probably gets vacuumed twice a day. Bird Brain knocks on a door. No special knock. I tense. Despite what Bird Brain said, his teammates could be hostile, or maybe Chainy is sitting on the other end, machine gun in each hand, just waiting to go Rambo on my skinny ass.

The door opens.

"Hello, I'm..."

"Not out here." I shoulder my way into a large sitting room and sigh. All those cameras make me twitchy as hell.

"Yes, I suppose that's wise." The man standing at the door is not what I expect...at all. Not Captain America, not Batman, not even Professor X. I stare at a chunky, balding guy who nervously adjusts his glasses and sticks a meaty hand out at me. He reminds me of one of those happy, white middle-aged guys that you only find in a Home Depot commercial. I can picture him cheerfully steering a riding mower as he gabs about all the outdoor projects he completed over the weekend thanks to Home Depot's great selection and amazing deals.

"Bear," he says.

"Gabe." I meant to say *Lee,* but oh well. Tarren can chew me a new asshole later if I ever find him again. I take Bear's sweaty hand. We shake and something about him puts me at ease. Underneath the chub, I think I see a fighter in him.

*Imminent bodily shutdown in...12 minutes*

My best friend, Chainy lounges in the corner, stroking his chain belt in a very unsettling manner. The evidence of our little scuffle is really starting to show. His nose looks twice the size it was before my fist introduced itself, and his left eye is beginning to swell and color. If he had Cyclopes's power, the glare he's giving me would burn a hole right through my chest.

*Nice to see you again too, you douche.*

"We have a lot of questions," Bear says, "but I think you deserve to have yours answered first."

I gratefully sink into a plushy chair, trying hard to control my descent so it isn't obvious that my legs are buckling. As Bear fills me in on some more of the Totem's background, I catch Bird Brain's eye and motion for my bag. When he brings it over,

I grab a can of Monster and gratefully pour more caffeine into my body. The pleasant British voice in my head warning me of imminent bodily shutdown backs off.

Bear keeps the Totem's origin story short and typically cryptic. Apparently everyone on the team had some encounter with an angel. I look around the room at each face – Bird Brain, Chainy, and Bear – and wonder how bad it was. The answer is obvious. Satan's gonads bad. Any student of comic books knows that the best heroes rise out of a primordial ooze of pain, betrayal, loss, and blood. Uncle Ben got capped right in front of Peter Parker's eyes. The Punisher's entire family was blown away, and, of course, little Bruce Wayne got to enjoy a blood shower courtesy of his parents' bullet-riddled bodies. Makes sense that enough angels wipe out enough innocents and certain people are going to turn the blackness of loss into something more than a memorial Facebook page.

The way Bear explains it, the dead guy, Puma got the ball rolling by posting on some whacky conspiracy theory message boards. That's where Bear discovered him. I watch Bear's big hands massage each other as he carefully skirts around his personal angel encounter of the third kind.

"I went to the police, of course," he sighs, "told them my story. They were less than receptive."

"Not a surprise. Cops aren't good for anything," I tell him. I decide not to mention that Bear's lucky his report got ignored. The angel network is breaking down, but there are still plenty of baddies in the government, in the corner offices of posh companies, and clinging to some pretty high rungs. There was a time when even asking certain questions could win you an instant trip to the morgue.

"I wanted answers...needed answers," Bear continues. His solution? The internet of course. His queries eventually took him to Puma's message board posts. Right alongside stories of alien probes, Big Foot sightings, and Tooth Fairy encounters, Bear found angels...in a manner of speaking. He and Puma chatted online.

"We discovered enough commonalities in our stories that I was confident we had been accosted by similar creatures," Bear says. His voice takes on a hint of excitement. "Imagine discovering that you aren't alone. That you aren't crazy. That something...some grand conspiracy truly does exist just beneath the surface of the life you thought you knew."

Makes me think back to all the civvies we've saved in the past. Over the years, certain people have gotten quite the eyeful. I wonder how they've been coping. Lo's strategy, apparently, is to poke out all the memories of his dad with metal hoops and studs.

Here's where Bear's story gets more interesting. He invited Puma over, presumably for tea, biscuits, knitting tips, and angel talk. Puma showed up in leather jacket, animal mask, and with a sidekick in tow named Finch.

At the mention of Finch's name, everyone glances toward the closed bedroom door. Bear continues the story.

"Puma had big plans for tracking down these creatures. He invited me to join the cause, as it were," Bear says dryly.

As it were. Love this guy.

"So, don't tell me," I say, "you immediately started sewing your superhero costumes."

"Of course not." Bear removes his glasses and carefully cleans each lens with a small cloth he pulls from his pocket.

"We were dangerously uninformed, unprepared."

Hmmmm, a man after Tarren's own heart.

"But I needed answers, and the authorities weren't willing to help."

Wow, when he puts it like that I realize that I actually understand where he's coming from. *Wouldn't I have nutted up, grabbed some guns, and done the same?*

"We needed to capture one of them," Bear says. "Then we could begin to understand what they were, their physiological differences from humans, their needs, their network. We could use this information to develop a strategy to fight."

Solid, through and through. I can't help myself, I'm starting to feel the first strands of a bro-crush on Bear. Just as he opens his mouth to go on with his story, my phone purrs in my pocket. Oh thank Frodo's disgusting, hairy feet. Tarren finally pulled his head out of his ass, or, even better, Maya decided to hand me an invite to her little angel massacre soiree.

"Hey," I say roughly into the phone.

"Hellloooo," a cheerful female voice sings.

...The hell?

"How much is the truck? My son saw it and fell in love with..."

"Thirty thousand," I blurt out.

"WHAT?" No more sing-song voice.

I hold up a finger to Bear, and turn my face away from the group. "It's one of a kind. Haunted."

"Uh..."

"You see, I hit a raccoon last month. Don't worry, no damage to the truck, at least no physical damage. But the thing is, I can feel its spirit inside the truck now. The raccoon, that is.

Like this angry, feral presence. Sometimes when I'm driving, this need comes over me to eat out of trashcans. That has to be the raccoon, right? So, I figured, hell, I don't want a truck haunted by a raccoon, but I bet someone in world would, right? So that's why I...hello?"

The dial tone buzzes in my ear. I tuck my phone in my pocket and look back to Bear. "You were saying?"

To his credit, Bear only raises an eyebrow before he continues. While Puma fumed in his pretty leather jacket, Bear threw himself into the task of figuring out an angel detection method. At about that point, serendipity happened in the form of a bloody catastrophe in Poughkeepsie, New York.

When Bear says the word "Poughkeepsie," it hits my spine with all the grace and delicacy of an ice pick.

He explains that a group of local teens disappeared from a nightclub only to be rescued from a putrid barn six days later. Of the eighteen that disappeared, only eleven made it out alive. The ones who were coherent enough blabbered about psychedelic drugs, a deranged cult, glowing hands, and chains.

I keep my mouth cemented shut. Yeah, I happen to know a thing or two about that particular incident in Poughkeepsie. If I wanted to rummage around in my memories, I could pull up the horror show we found when we opened up that barn door. I suck in a quick breath as I see all those kids rotting away, chained together inside horse stalls. The smell, I'll never forget the smell, or how the flies crawled over the open, glassy eyes of the dead. Just teenagers, all of them. It was enough to make me wish I could've revived the angels who snacked on those teens just so I could kill them all over again, this time with honey and fire ants.

I tune back into Bear's story. "Puma and I found similarities in the stories of the teens and what we had experienced, particularly regarding energy absorption through the hands. We were able to track down several of the survivors to garner more details." He gaze moves to Bird Brain and then to Chainy.

That's when it finally clicks. "You're the one Tarren saved," I say to Chainy. Technically, Maya dragged his ass out of a burning house, but Tarren CPR'd the hell out of him until he had no choice but to start breathing again. Tarren has that effect on people.

It's like I flipped some kind of switch in Chainy and all his feelings come rushing back into him. He literally jumps up from the floor, belt clanging. His eyes are intense. "You know him? The man with the scar?"

Oops, probably shouldn't have dropped Tarren's name like that. He's really big into not telling complete amateurs our true identities.

"I know him," I hedge. "We were all there that day. Me, Tarren, and M-Buffy. We took care of those angels and called the authorities to rescue you." And maybe some of that psychedelic cult stuff was my fault, but it wasn't exactly easy to throw together a good cover story in the midst of that horror show.

I hear a groan and look over at Bird Brain who seems to either be experiencing serious gas pains or partaking in an unpleasant realization. "She was...there to rescue us?" he finally manages.

I stare at him. "Yep."

Bear is staring at me, and I have the feeling he would like to unscrew the top of my head, stab a straw through my brain, and suck out every ounce of information I have about the angels. But he keeps himself in check.

"Chain and Penguin wanted to join our cause," he continues. "Their information was substantive. We believe these creatures feed from the life force of humans through a mechanism in their hands. They possess great strength and speed and the ability to create fire."

Not too shabby. When Tarren and I rained down bullets on the group of angels in Poughkeepsie, one of the wings started spouting fire. Chainy and Bird Brain were in the room at the time. Makes sense that they would jump to this conclusion.

"Angels have different abilities," I tell them. "Fire is one we see a lot."

The rest is history. The team came together. Course, they sat around for a couple of months trying and failing to flush out any angels and making that adorably wretched video in a bid to warn the world of its impending doom. But, it turns out, Bird Brain isn't as dumb as he seems. Apparently he hit on the same realization that I did – angels would need to continuously move to avoid detection, and vulnerable areas would offer the safest human buffet option. They wound up here, in Peoria Fucking Illinois.

This is when Bear blows my world and forever cements my bro-crush. Bird Brain noticed that when the angels in Poughkeepsie touched him their hands were cold. Bear extrapolated (his word) that angels might have a lower core body temperature than humans. He put his theory to the test by setting up small heat sensing cameras all over Peoria.

He beckons me over to a desk where I see a laptop monitor split into eight tiles. Each shows a different darkened outdoor view. One camera broadcasts a parking lot. I watch bundled humans jog from their cars, each lit in bright whites.

Ho-Ly Shit! Did amateur hour just get serious? Distinguishing angels from humans was one of the most challenging parts of the job before Maya came along with her weird spidey sense for angels. If we could have been using heat sensor goggles the entire time, or, better yet, done Bear's camera trick, we could have saved ourselves boatloads…no aircraft carrier loads of time and effort and probably saved a few extra lives in the bargain.

I give Bear a curt nod of approval as I stare at his laptop and try not to drool. No need to give him a big head about an idea I'm totally going to steal.

The rest of the story I already know from Bird Brain. Bear made several sightings of possible angels around the city, but his team was unable to converge quickly enough until they discovered an angel feeding on a cop in the alley. By the time the team was in place, the original angel had taken off, but Maya was kind enough to show up and give them a second chance at angel nabbing.

"We shouldn't have treated her the way we did," Bear says apologetically. "She didn't kill the police officer. When I reviewed the footage, it's clear that she was going after the first creature. When we spoke, she was…different from the other experience that I had."

I ignore his apology so I'm not tempted to kick my new friend in the balls. "The other angel you captured, you think she's trying to use him to find their home base?"

Bear nods. "She took possession of one of our tranq guns. She could have easily tranqed him and brought him to a different location for questioning."

*Or she could have gone angel undercover like in Texas.* That was the mission right before Grand took Tarren...before I almost ended up on a permanent sabbatical six feet under. My heart pounds in my chest. Maya knew Tarren would institute full Styx protocol as soon as she was taken by Animal Farm over here.

I lean over, elbows planted on my knees. Maya is all alone out there, tip-toeing into a pit of vipers. I need to find her. Fast. Doesn't matter that my bones feel heavy as lead coated in more lead. I can rest the next time I die.

# *Chapter 15*

Montage time. Sir Hopsalot scurries around the plush hotel room, while I set up my laptop and let my fingers fly. I've got an enemy. An iPhone. Not exactly a Cylon or Dalek, but it'll have to do.

This is the phone The Totem took off the angel they captured. Somewhere in its circuits I might be able to dig out information on Maya's whereabouts. Look at that – bulging muscles need not apply. Good old hacking is what I need to get all day-saving up in here.

*You wanna go?* I think to the phone as it leers at me with its password screen. I find a compatible USB port in my bag o' tricks and hook it to Starbuck. My girl zaps the hell out of the phone with a couple handy software bugs before its password window dissolves with a whimper. The welcome screen greets me like a happy puppy. Call me Gabe "Phone Whisperer" Fox.

Now the hard part. I chew the inside of my mouth. I've never put a trace on a call before. Give me a few days and an unlimited supply of Monster energy drinks, and I can teach myself just about anything techy, but the bad guys aren't exactly going to play nice while I get my advanced hackers degree from the Black Hat University of Phoenix.

*If Maya gets caught. If they discover who she really is....*

So not helping right now, brain. I need to put cement flippers on those thoughts and throw them into the Hudson. I take a deep, cleansing breath, like the kind they teach in yoga. On my right, Bear sits uncomfortably in one of the plush chairs, monitoring his video feeds. Bird Brain is on the couch now, watching me dick around with the phone. And Chainy, I definitely need to keep my eye on him. I find him scrunched in the corner scribbling in some kind of journal, probably writing the world's worst angst poetry.

I interlace my fingers, stretch them, and feel the pleasant pops that always drive Maya insane. Okay, desperate times...desperate measures. Time to eat shit.

I jump online through Tor and quickly dive past the legit part of the internet into the darkness where the depraved, the misunderstood, and the true baddies lurk. Tor cloaks my IP as I swim among the sharks. Hackers. They may have been outcasts in high school, but as the world shifts more of its treasures into ones and zeroes, these ghosts in the machine are demi-gods.

I visit some old stomping grounds – an exclusive hacker message board that I cracked into a few years ago. LuvDragon is online. I take another cleansing breath. *Here we go.* As soon as I message her, Starbuck freezes. I don't even want to know how LuvDragon got another back door into my computer. After I found the last one I amped up virus protection and sweeps with the equivalent of computer steroids, but LuvDragon still found a way in. I can only imagine what she's doing right now, combing through Starbuck's entire memory, reviewing every single site I've accessed, all my files.

On a normal day, LuvDragon is so paranoid I bet she owns a pet monkey who tastes her food. All hackers are twitchy like that. Long absences do not make her heart grow fonder. If there's even a whiff you got picked up and turned by the Feds, MI6, or any other agency, these guys will fry you. In the opinion of yours truly, keyboards are way scarier than nuclear bombs.

For 30 long, long minutes my screen stays frozen. I hunch over my laptop, slurp down another can of Monster, and try to look busy. I type in nonsense, staring intently at the screen as if I'm actually doing something so my team doesn't realize that a girl living in a basement in South Korea has me totally by the balls.

I wonder what LuvDragon will make of the Google maps I've put together and labeled with meaningless numerals or my Google Alerts set up to comb through obits across the country. She'll also see the Pirate Bay files of my fav music and shows. And the porn. She'll see that too, but it's probably tame compared to what she dabbles in.

She won't get much more than that from Starbuck. I keep all the important stuff on an external hard drive at home protected with every single encryption invented by man. Starbuck doesn't hold anything personal, nothing about the mission, no pics, not even my chats with Amanda.

Just as I wonder if LuvDragon has sucked everything out of my computer and decided she doesn't want to come out and play, my screen resets. New wallpaper of Lizbeth Salander. Cute. There's LuvDragon on Skype, her leather-clad avatar berating me for going dark for the past four months. "Cocksucker" is the closest she gets to a term of endearment. I let her go on and on and on, impressed by the vividness and variety of her threats. Then it's time to lay on the charm. I go hard. My fingers tap out roses and sunsets into the chat box. Then I go to places that are darker and wetter and sting in a good way.

I can tell I'm softening her up when she stops listing my own body parts that will soon be up my ass if I disappear again. You don't ask favors of these people, so I present what I need from her like a challenge. I start by casually asking if she's still the hottest hacker chick on the net. She's got a complex about that, and I rile her up good.

The idea of hacking a phone company to triangulate a call definitely appeals to her deviant side. LuvDragon is half noble in her quest to punish the wicked and half anarchist, thrilling in her ability to tear the shit out of the people and companies she doesn't like. This girl can get into places you wouldn't believe – banks, hospitals, senior government email accounts. I've also seen her rip people to shreds even within our group. If she finds out someone's gotten turned, she'll unmask them, post their social security numbers, their addresses, and their credit card number. Hell, she might even post their first grade report card or the secret poem about bed wetting they wrote and deleted twenty years ago.

In other words, she's a stick of dynamite. I know that if I don't dance just right, I won't just get burned, I'll get exploded into a thousand, thousand pieces. And then she'll probably piss on all the meat confetti.

LuvDragon wants more details of the mission. Who am I tracking and why? This is dangerous. I want her off the scent. In the past, I've actually considered cluing her into the whole evil angels taking over America thing. I bet she could be a helluva crime fighter even within the confines of her dungeon, but she's too unstable. I wouldn't be surprised if she turned tail, got herself angelfied, and cackled madly while she started amassing a body count.

After copious amounts of flattering, teasing, and lying, LuvDragon is on board. She makes me promise to help with some crazy scheme to post sweatshop videos on Nike's YouTube channel, and I agree to all of it. Three hours she tells me and she'll have the phone company bent over her knee begging for more. I give her the number on my burner to text when she's ready and then place the phone in Bird Brain's care.

As soon as I switch Starbuck's wallpaper back to this smokin' hot pic of Kiera Knightley, I realize that I'm in bad, bad shape. I can barely hold my head up, and my entire body just wants to crumble into dust. I can practically feel my atoms groaning under the strain of having to hold themselves together.

I know that The Totem has a thousand and one questions for me, especially Bear with his sharp beady eyes, but I think I just lost my grasp of the English language. I mumble some excuse about needing to meditate or something like that. Let them think I'm a higher level being or whatever.

I drag myself to the bedroom and close the door behind me. I couldn't tell you what color the comforter is, but this is the most wonderful, gorgeous bed I have ever seen in my life. I stumble toward it and then my eyes fall on a small hump under the covers.

Someone is in the bed; someone small, almost drowning under the covers. I walk to the side of the bed where she curls right on the edge. Shiny black eyes stare at me from beneath puffy lids. Long black hair frames her bronze face.

"You're Finch," I say, remembering how everyone's gaze flicked to the bedroom when Bear said her name. The girl doesn't respond. I know the look on her face, the hollow pits of her eyes.

Against my will I'm flashing back four years ago to that grungy alley in Madison, Wisconsin, to the black Ford, to Tarren slumped against the wheel, dried blood flaking off his neck. He'd called me from a payphone – that's how I found him – and whispered a single word. *Styx.* I want to bury that word, drown it in acid, burn it until even the ashes disintegrate.

I didn't realize at first how bad it was, how many ribbons Grand cut through Tarren. But when I got him out of the driver's seat and saw all the blood soaked into the leather...And his face. It wasn't just the cut slicing open his skin from ear to chin, but his empty eyes. A light gone, forever gone.

He didn't even have to tell me. I knew Tammy was dead.

I push those images away like they were diseased. It's been four years since that day, but the memories are so fresh I can almost smell the blood. Tarren's eyes still hold that hollow space where Tammy once lived.

I find myself still looking into the girl's round face, that utter emptiness. What am I going to do if Maya gets hurt, if she dies, if she's already dead? I can't lose anyone else. If anything happened to Maya or Tarren, I think I'd walk off a cliff or grab a bottle and never let go.

Breathe.

Breathe.

Breathe.

The exhaustion helps the fear drift way.

"Do you mind if I take a nap on the other side of the bed?" I ask the girl. She blinks but says nothing. Sounds like permission to me. I crawl onto the other side of the bed. I should stay on top of the covers, but the thick comforter feels so warm, and I'm shivering worse than the ancient rust bucket I pulled up in. It dawns on me as I slip under the covers that I should have taken off my shoes. Too late now.

I lay down. *Ohhhhhh, Heaven.* So much hangs in the balance, but I need the world to be still for just an hour. Maya is strong and smart and has made crazy progress in all her training. She also has a knack for thinking like Tarren.

*Just hang on for another few hours. I'm coming, I promise,* I think, hoping some mystical force in the universe will send my thoughts to her.

Something comes over me. Maybe I've lost all my senses to exhaustion, but I scooch over, crossing the invisible line between my side of the bed and the girl's side. I feel her sadness, like a magnet, drawing me closer, kindling my memories of Tammy and my fear for what might happen to Maya.

After Tammy died, I worked so hard to make Tarren smile while he was recovering. I told him every joke I knew and wrote a thousand new ones at night. I wove wild stories, each one funnier than the last. I went down on my knees, bawling, begging him to smile even if it wasn't real. I hate those memories. Hate remembering him wrapped in all those bandages. Eyes like ice.

Without even asking permission, I draw the girl in my arms. Her body is limp and small and warm.

"I'm sorry," I tell her. "I lost my mom and my sister."

I kind of expect her to scream or kick me in the balls, but she turns her head, resting it against my chest. "You can hit me if I snore," I say, hoping that she'll laugh. No laugh, but she snuggles closer, and it feels good. I fall asleep with her soft hair on my cheek.

# Chapter 16

No dreams. Just an earthquake. I come to slowly, the world swirling around me and a heavy grip on my shoulder.

"I think something's wrong with him," a voice says over me. My body shakes. For a moment I think it's another seizure. I got to ride that delightful rollercoaster twice the first week I was back at home after the coma. I've been up against some scary shit in my day, but nothing like losing control of your body, blacking out, and coming to with piss soaked jeans and Maya staring over me, her eyes the size of dinner plates.

Then I realize the seizure is actually Bird Brain shaking me.

"Stop, stop," I groan, trying to collect my thoughts. They've wandered quite afield. "I'm alive." *Probably.*

Bird Brain gives me a look like he isn't quite sure. If cells had voices, every single one in my body would be begging me to close my eyes and pull the covers over my head. But Maya. Pit of vipers.

Batman doesn't hit the snooze button.

I sit up with effort. One hand goes up to smooth my hair, but the bristles remind me that I don't have much left. I look around and realize that Finch isn't in the bed with me. I probably creeped her out for life with that unannounced cuddle. Might've turned her off of men entirely.

"Text come through?" I say, trying to project an air of smooth confidence and not trip on the sheets at the same time. The concerned expression on Bird Brain's face tells me that he's not buying what I'm selling. Chainy leans against the doorframe, arms folded across his chest. *Thanks for not stabbing me through the eye with a butter knife while I slept,* I think to him as I walk past.

"Here," Bird Brain hands over my phone as we enter into the main room. Sir Hopsalot digs into his tub of hay in the corner. I don't even remember setting it up and wonder if one of my new teammates did me a solid.

The phone contains a single text. Ready.

"Nice." I hold out my fist to Bear as I pass him. Confusion clouds his face, but then his knuckles meet mine. He smiles a little, and I grin back at him.

"Come along, Pond, we have work to do," I tell him. It's a guess, but his eyes light up, and I know why I instantly clicked with him. We *Doctor Who* crazies have to stick together. I sit behind the desk and confirm with LuvDragon that I'm ready on my end. She gives me the green light. She's hacked the phone company. When I make an outgoing call, she'll be able to follow the signal relay and give me a location on the other end.

I feel the eyes from the Totem members boring into me like three sets of diamond tipped drills. Got to impress. I almost smile as I scroll through the phone's call log. I'm looking for someone the angel calls often, someone who has the highest chance of being an angel in his group. If he or she is at their home base when I call, then we'll be golden...if I can keep the call going long enough. A lot of "ifs", which reminds me...

I spot my lucky hat near my bag and get that on my head pronto. I can practically feel its good juju start flowing through me.

Names slide down the screen as I scroll – Rachel, Nick, Mom, Sam, Malcolm, Diamond, Heather, Danielle, Stephanie. Wait...wait...*WOOZER*! I scroll back up to Heather.

Not only has our angel called her about a thousand million times, but in her profile pic Heather wears a bikini that leaves only the exact shade of her nipples to the imagination. I can barely punch her number into my burner phone. God it'd be a shame to have to kill her today and take those breasts out of existence.

The phone rings on the other end. I realize that about now would be a decent time to come up with a...

"Hello?" Her voice is a like a bell, soft and promising.

"What the hell you doing to me Janice?" I scream at her. "You bitch, I loved you! I...I...loved you." My voice cracks right on cue.

"What?"

"Don't *what* me. Sheryl done told me yous was grinding all over Manuel at the reception. Manuel. He's my step-da for godsake!"

"Wait, wait, I think you got the wrong number." She giggles nervously. "Who is this?"

I love the Southern in her voice. Every word sounds like crawdads, Budweiser, and deer season. I look at the clock running on the computer. I've got to keep her on the hook for at least two minutes.

"Don't play with me, Janice. Why you doing this?" My

voice is a whimper.

"I'm Heather," Heather responds back. "I don't know no Janice." I hear her muffle the phone for a second. "Don't know," she responds to a question outside my hearing. "Wrong number I think."

*Don't hang up. Don't hang up. Please God, I'll tattoo Jesus on my neck if she doesn't hang up right now.*

"Hello? Hello?" I holler into the phone.

"Look-e-here," she comes back with a sigh, "ya got the wrong number."

"You for real?" I say, my voice immediately soft and grave.

"Uh-huh."

I glance at the clock. One minute to go. "Figures she wouldn't give me her real number. I was such a fool. She's probably laughing at me right now, if her mouth ain't already full of Manuel's…" I cut off with a sob.

Silence stretches on the other side of the line. *Please don't hang up. God, you kept me alive for a reason. It sure as shit wasn't to lose Maya.*

"What's yer name?" Heather asks.

"Sal," I tell her, "though I guess it should be Sap."

"Nah, don't say that. Sal, I'm sorry yer girl ain't been faithful. That's real low of her." The phone gets muffled again. "I will. Just give me a minute here. Sal's got some troubles."

What a sweetheart. I look up to the three faces staring at me. Bird Brain and Bear are severely impressed. Chainy, well, I think I could shove a rainbow up his ass and he'd still look like he was forced to eat broccoli for dinner every day of his life.

"She wasn't really my girl," I sniffle. "We were only together one night, but I thought…Heather, do you believe in love at first sight?" The clock hits the two minute mark, but brevity is Tarren's thing. I gotta show these newbies that it's okay to enjoy the job, at least a little.

"Course I do!" Heather responds, her voice practically squeaking with enthusiasm. I can only imagine how many times this girl has watched *Love Actually*. "Sal, that girl, whatshername, don't you worry 'bout her. She sounds like a bitch, anyway."

"I just..." I breathe heavily into the phone. "Sometimes I don't think I'm gonna find love. You know, like it's just not in the cards for me."

"You can't think like that, Sal," Heather insists. "You sound like a great guy. You just gotta keep trying. You know, sometimes life can be...can give us some rotten tomatoes, but that don't mean the sun ain't coming out tomorrow."

*What?* "Yeah, guess you're right," I mutter.

"Ya gonna find love, Sal, I know ya are," Heather says with ardent enthusiasm.

I hear a bang on her end of the phone. "Who the hell you talking to?" a tinny voice yells.

"No one, wrong number," Heather answers, her voice far away like she's holding the phone to her side.

"Hang up, get naked, and get on the god damn bed!" the voice growls.

*Whoa, what the hell is going on over there?*

"Heather, you still there?" I say, wondering if I'm going to get slapped with a dial tone.

"Sal? Sorry, hon, I gotta go." Her voice is hurried, and I catch a hint of a nervousness that I don't like. "I'll pray for ya, Sal. I'll ask God to put a good woman in your path."

"Can you ask the big guy to make her as kind and beautiful as you?"

Heather giggles. "Bye," she whispers. A voice screams from her end of the call, "I SAID GET OFF THE—" The call cuts out. I set the phone down and give a little bow to my audience.

"What was that?" Bird Brain asks.

"Art. True art," I tell him and spin the chair around to my open laptop. LuvDragon already has an address in our chat window. Bingo, Yahtzee, and Connect Four! I type it into Google Maps and come up with some suburb on the edge of town.

We got 'em. I am at record awesome levels today. If Maya were here I'd offer to let her kiss my feet, and she'd stick her tongue out at me, or pretend to gag, or just smile and call me an idiot savant in the nicest way possible.

"What now?" Bear asks, peering over my shoulder at the map and the little red line that takes us from our swanky hotel room to the battlefield.

I turn my chair around to make sure I have their attention. "Now we shoot people."

# Chapter 17

My pronouncement doesn't exactly go over well, unless you count Chainy. His eyes gleam with an unsettling anticipation. The kid is a therapist's wet dream, I swear. Bear is uneasy and Bird Brain...without meaning to, I actually glance down at his crotch to make sure we don't need a cleanup in aisle five.

I give him a questioning look, and he surprises me again by squaring his shoulders. I see a little resolve start mixing with all that fear on his face. Guess I should stop discounting the guy. He wouldn't be here if there wasn't a spine somewhere in his lanky body.

"Okay," he says. "Okay, how do we do that?"

"Do you guys have guns?"

"Only tranquilizers," Bear admits.

"I have a gun," Chainy says, clearly proud but trying to play it cool. Leave it to the crazy one to be armed.

"That gun doesn't happen to be registered in your name though, right?" I ask. "Or anyone related to you, because it would be downright stupid to commit a crime with a registered gun."

Chainy shuts the hell up.

I honestly think about leaving right then and there. When I look at my new team all I see are big glowing Ls on each forehead, which can equally stand for "Loser" or "Liability". I feel the echoes of a migraine starting in my brain. What choice do I have? Can I really go up against an entire group of angels on my own? If anything, the Gabettes can at least provide a distraction. I don't even know how many angels we're dealing with, and Maya might somehow be in the mix.

The beat of pain grows louder inside my skull. Much as I hate to admit this, I need Tarren right now. Regardless of the fact that he might be more robot than man on occasion, he always knows how to play each situation. Also, doesn't hurt that I can trust him with my life every time.

"So we have an address," Bear says, breaking through my pity party. "I suggest we set up cameras, confirm that we're dealing with these creatures, or angels as you call them, establish their numbers, and try to determine movement patterns that we can exploit."

Whoa, did Tarren's ghost just invade Bear's body? I could have sworn he and my brother just had a Vulcan Mind Meld.

"That's a great plan, Yogi," I tell Bear, "except they have my sister, and seeing as the weather is breaking, they'll probably be packing their evil suitcases right now, ready to move on. No, we have to shoot them. All of them."

"Yogi?"

I wait a second, hoping that he'll get it. Blank stares all around. I look to Sir Hopsalot, who lies stretched on his belly under the desk. *Seriously, right?* I think to the bunny.

"Cause you're smarter than the average bear," I sigh.

"Why we still talking? Let's go," Chainy urges and touches his belt. I really, really don't want to know what he does with that thing after hours.

"Crazy is right," I snap to the Gabettes as I close my laptop and start shoveling my tech into my bag. "We'll find an abandoned warehouse, get a little weapons training, and then it's go time."

"You have a plan?" Bear asks. He's not mean about it, but I hear the underlying question. *Are we going to live through this thing?*

"Course I have a plan," I scoff at him. I crouch on the floor, and Sir Hopsalot comes bounding to me. At least one person in this room trusts me wholeheartedly. I stroke his velvet-soft ears and then put him into his carrying case. I pack up the rest of his supplies, and when I stand up, three pairs of eyes follow me.

"You mind sharing the plan with the rest of us?" Bear asks, again not unkindly.

"Not yet." I give him a grin big enough to hide my fear. "First, we need a montage!"

***

Before our awesome training montage can really get going, we need a montage-friendly facility. Chainy seems to know his way around town. He and Bird Brain take the truck, while I putter behind them in the Bug with Bear as my copilot.

Man, the guy asks a lot of questions. I try to get him into a debate about which Doctor he likes best – the classic opener in any Whovian meet and greet – but he keeps getting off track, wanting to know how angels are made, about the different abilities we've seen, how we hunt them.

I give him the most important info, but I'm careful about

letting too many details slip. Tarren wouldn't like me spilling the beans, even to an okay dude like Bear. If any of his crew are captured – a scenario that, let's be honest, isn't exactly unlikely – they could give up our methods and compromise our hunting ability.

"You just gotta shoot 'em," I tell Bear again. "Head or heart, though head is easier. They die just like everybody else." I look over at Bear. His clenched jaw tells me this info is going down about as easily as cold spinach, but he nods for me to continue. "Killing really isn't the hard part," I say as I slow for a stoplight. "The real trick is not getting caught. You've got to be really careful about that."

*Funny, weren't Maya and I having this same convo just a few days ago?*

"And how does one get away with murder?" Bear asks, just a tad of a tremble in his voice.

"Whoa, it ain't murder if we're talking about evil dudes. Murder is like taking out kittens and children and grammys. Big, big difference."

Bear is quiet for a moment. The Bug's engine whines in the silence. Finally he says, "What if a grandmother was turned into an angel?"

Jesus, now he sounds like Maya trying to paint gray all over what I consider to be pretty clear lines. "Then she's not a grammy anymore," I explain to Bear. "She's an evil dude. Damsel in distress privileges revoked. Right to end her, granted."

Bear stares at me. The glasses and frowny face make him look like a college professor about to scold me for a plagiarized term paper. "I see," is all he says.

Up ahead, the truck pulls into an empty, snow-logged parking lot. The Bug does not like this at all. She whines, and her wheels slip, but I nudge her in next to the truck. I step out and look around. A darkened building looms in front of us. Yes, this will do nicely. I don't see any headlights from the road. My flashlight beam finds a "For Lease" sign in the front window of the building. I can see the outline where letters used to hang proudly at the top of the building.

"This used to be a bridal warehouse or something," Chainy says. "Will it work?"

Big, empty, and away from civilization. "Oh yeah."

"It's not like they'd leave the door unlocked though," Bird Brain says.

I have to give him a pitying look for that. Without further acknowledging his dumbassery, I walk up to the door and sweep my flashlight around looking for cameras. None that I can see. No tracks in the snow. They don't have a guard. This place is good and truly abandoned. I reach into my inner pocket and pull out my lock pick kit.

Tarren may whip my ass up, down, and all the way to Sunday in martial arts. He may have a couple dozen IQ points on me. He may look way better in a pair of brightly-colored tights and a cape, but I can polish a lock like no one else.

The thick padlock on this door is a handsome son of a bitch, but he goes down just like all the rest before him. I get a wedge in there, pop up the pins, and I'm inviting my new friends out from the cold in a matter of minutes.

"You've got to teach me that," Bird Brain says, and yeah, I can't blame him for the clear admiration on his face. I can be pretty damn impressive sometimes.

I expect the place to be a desert, but a counter stands up front, and empty racks line the walls of a large inner room. Our feet echo loudly, and the thick shadows that crowd around our flashlight beams definitely dial up the creepy.

Chainy runs his hands along the wall, searching for lights.

"Don't," I tell him sharply.

"Why not?" It's too dark to see his expression, but I'm just going to assume he looks mighty pissed.

"Electrical use gets recorded," Bear says, "and someone might see the lights from the road."

Ahhh, the grasshopper learns quickly. I feel a tiny bit better about this team's chances for long-term survival.

"Wipe that down. Guys, no touching anything. No fingerprints," I call out. We set up a circle of flashlights against the wall, and I unzip my duffle bag. Inside are some very special ladies – three Glocks and one extra Berretta. Thank you Franklin and your stupid fluffy cat.

Chainy's eyes lovingly gaze at the spankin' new Bushmaster Carbon 15 rifle on my shoulder.

"Not a chance," I tell him. "This one is mine."

# *Chapter 18*

Our training montage is sad as fuck. In the dark warehouse, The Gabettes' motto becomes, "no matter how low the bar, we'll still find a way to trip over it." I guess I should be grateful that they at least know to hold the guns with the barrels pointing away from their faces.

Over two long hours we don't have, my lovable team of losers works on stance, aim, pulling back the safety trigger on the Glocks, and anticipating the recoil. I show them how to fill the magazine with bullets ("Press harder! Harder! Wrong way you igit."), how to push the mag into the guns, and how to drop the mag once it's empty. We don't shoot any live rounds. Who knows how far the sound will carry, and honestly, I don't trust these jokers not to accidentally shoot each other.

*Tarren, for the love of Xena's tits, where are you?*

The mannequin is an inspired find. Harley Quinn, as I dub her, stands a little lopsided, has nubs for hands, and willingly offers her creepy, stoic face for imaginary target practice. As I take the team through Mom's drills, I can almost hear her voice, "S*peed, speed, speed. Everything like clockwork, so practiced you don't even have to think about it. Your body just knows* *what to do."* We almost never have to shoot more than twice, but in those few instances where we have, dropping a mag and slamming in another in a fluid motion was critical. You drop the mag or jam it, and you're dead.

"You're dead!" I shout at Bird Brain and Bear and Chainy again and again when they are too slow, when they forget to pull the safety trigger, when they hold the gun too high, too low. "Dead! Dead! Dead!"

"This isn't a game!" God, how many times did Mom say that to me and Tammy when we were goofing off during practice or before a mission? *"It only takes one mistake, just one!"* she'd say, her voice low and hard. I understood back then that she was trying to save our lives, but my respect for her grows by leaps and bounds during this piss poor training. With every passing minute, I feel more responsible for the three guys in front of me as they fumble with their weapons.

Chainy is the swiftest, the most natural, but he keeps pulling the gun high and trying to shoot with one hand like he's some kind of movie hero.

"Two hands you dolt!" I tell him. "You won't hit the broad side of a barn with one hand."

The other two are awkward and unsure. Bear starts to get the hang of it, but his movements are slow and mechanical, like he has to carefully remember each step. I need fluid. I need muscle memory. If he has to think this hard in a quiet dark warehouse with a silent enemy standing still, what's going to happen when we're shooting live rounds, people are screaming, and arterial blood is squirting in his eyes? And Bird Brain, Jesus H. Christ, the kid needs a remedial gun class, the kind where they start with squirt guns.

After two hours, The Gabettes are exhausted and frustrated, and we're out of time. Every part of me wants to curl up in a corner and sleep for a week, but I can't leave Maya out there, not for a minute longer.

"One last thing guys," I tell them trying to push through the hoarseness in my voice. "When we get there, we'll be shooting. All of us. It's going to be loud. If you think you know how loud a gunshot is, you don't. Be ready for the noise. Stay steady. And pull the trigger. Just pull the god-damned trigger."

Not exactly a rousing speech for the troops, but no one's ever called me Shakespeare.

I lay out my brilliant plan. The team is silent as I speak. Bear's face seems to have collected more worry lines, Bird Brain looks like he's trying not to spew chunks, and Chainy is all pent-up energy, ready to spray crazy at the first opportunity. I think *Holy God, they actually trust me, and they're probably going to die for it.*

***

I take lead in the whining rust bucket as we drive through the darkness to the address LuvDragon traced from my call with the lovely Heather. I shove a protein bar in my mouth, hoping the calories will somehow infuse me with magical healing energy. A lot of unhappy thoughts rattle in my head. What if Maya is already...*shit*. What if there are dozens of angels? What if they surround us? What if one of them unleashes a power I've never seen before, something I can't prepare for? What if this plan is so stupid that even General Custer would call me crazy, reckless, and an ass hat of the first degree?

In the passenger seat, Bird Brain looks straight out the window, and his lips move silently. I wonder if he's praying.

Maybe I should pray too. I'm not really the church going type, but I believe in God and Heaven. Have to. The thought of never seeing Tammy again or Mom just isn't even worth contemplating. And my dad will be up there too. Even though I don't remember him, I think a part of me is empty, missing all the jokes and laughs and father bonding stuff we would have shared.

Okay, so I'll write my own Hallmark Channel made-for-TV movie later. It's time to focus. Be all commando and leader-like. I look at my passenger again and notice that his hands tremble in his lap. Hell, he might have an aneurism before we even get to any shooting. I hand him one of the remaining protein bars stuffed in the cup holder between us. He takes it automatically.

"You're an idiot," I tell him.

"Huh?" He turns to look at me.

"Your superhero name can't be Penguin. Penguin is a Batman villain." I honestly can't believe I even have to explain this to him.

He shrugs. "I know, but I didn't think it was a big deal."

Is this guy serious? Does he have any respect whatsoever for the vast and beautiful world of shit-tastic comics?

"Penguin is a well-established villain in the D.C. Universe. You don't take someone else's villain name or superhero name. That's crime fighting 101, Son."

"But..."

"And the villain you chose is a total joke. Penguin is a fat diabetes factory, and I'm pretty sure he has a very unnatural relationship with his penguin pets. For God's sake man, his weapon is an umbrella. Not a big deal my ass! As soon as we finish this mission and rescue my sister, you're getting a new name. Something like…like…" I look him up and down, "Beanpole."

"Beanpole?" He looks at me aghast. "That's not even an animal."

"Beanpole, hmmmm, has the power to be tall and gangly. Defeats his enemies by reaching up to high storage shelves and dropping jumbo cans of tomato sauce from Costco on their heads."

I actually glance in the rearview mirror, ready to trade knowing smirks with Maya. My heart pangs hard when I gaze at the empty back seat.

"Not what you expected, is it?" I ask Penguin, softening my voice so he knows I've let the whole name fiasco slide for now.

"None of it is. Six months ago my sister was alive and I didn't know any of this. Yesterday I thought all of those things were evil and that no one was doing anything to fight them. And now this. You. Buffy."

This is the first time I'm hearing about the dead sister. I immediately feel like someone put my heart in a clamp. I almost want to tell him about Tammy, about how her death shredded me up so bad that the only thing keeping me from marrying a bottle of gin was that Tarren was so much worse. I have to believe I salvaged enough of him that the rest will come back when he's ready.

"You should eat that. Calories," I tell Penguin, nodding to the unopened protein bar in his hand.

He turns it over in his hand, glances at the ingredient list, and then puts the bar back in the cup holder. "Peanut allergy," he says.

"Sucks man," I manage, but in my head, all I can think is,

*We're all so going to die.*

When we're a quarter mile out from the address, I pull off to the side of the road and look around. We've left the main city of Peoria behind and entered into a quiet, sleeping area of vast lawns and giant houses that sit far back from the road. Some of them have their own gates. Dawn is just starting to break over the horizon. I look around and decide that this is as good a place to start as any other. No one should notice the cars for at least a few hours, which will be more than enough time to get Maya or get dead.

When I climb out of the Bug, Penguin reluctantly follows. I take a moment to breath in the cold air and stare at the shapes of two lumpy snowmen on the lawn in front of me. In the growing light, I can see that the taller snowman proudly shows off a stick mohawk, four eyes, and a plastic sword tied to its branch hand. Pretty cool. Makes me think of Mandy, probably tucked away in bed dreaming nice dreams. I wonder if our tragic little snowman is still in front of her apartment building with his fuzzy pink scarf and mismatched stick arms.

I hear steps behind me. My team is gathering round. Bringing the Gabettes with me is probably an epic mistake. I know Tarren would think so. Tammy would too. If I were even at fifty percent, I'd go in alone and take my chances, but the truth is, this quarter mile walk through the snow is going to take about every ounce of energy I have left. Who the hell knows if I'll even be able to hit anything? But these guys came to Peoria Fucking Illinois to fight, and I'm gonna give 'em one.

***

We trek silently, my flashlight sweeping ahead as we walk single file along the side of the road. The sniper rifle on my back thuds softly feeling like it weighs a thousand pounds and then some. The horizon is smoky gray as the coming sun beats back the night. I hear someone stumble. My money's on Penguin, but I don't look back to check. If I stop for one moment, I'm pretty sure I'm going to lie down in the snow and die.

The adrenaline comes slowly. There isn't much, but I'll take it. When we come to the driveway of the huge mansion that matches my address, I stop. Time for a big speech. Not going to lie, I've always dreamed of giving a rousing speech to troops in the face of impossible odds, but I can't exactly scream, "but they'll never take...OUR FREEDOM!" or "TODAY IS NOT THAT DAY!" without waking up every angel within a fifteen block radius. Also, I don't have a horse, which really is a key part of rousing speeches.

"Okay guys, listen up," I say. The Gabettes look at me, their faces expectant. "On the way here I called Beanpole an idiot." I nod towards Penguin. "Truth is, we're all idiots and most likely a little crazy. Normal people wouldn't be out here freezing their asses off, trying to take down an army of super humans. But we're here, and we've all got our reasons. We each had a choice to make, and we chose crazy." I swallow. Usually, words come as easily as breathing to me, but these words are hard and sticky. "I am asking a lot of you tonight. I am asking you to put your life on the line. I'm asking you to pull the trigger. I'm asking you to kill someone if you have to. So, I guess, I just wanted to say thank you. I'm going to do my best to keep you safe, but I won't...can't make any promises. We could all die. You need to know that. If you want to walk away, then..."

"God, shut up," Chainy groans. "We all get it. We're not leaving. Just tell us where to go."

Not exactly the roaring adulation I'd hoped for, but Chainy is right. It's freezing out here, and we're going to get spotted if we just linger in front of the driveway. I swallow the ball busting comment I have for Chainy and just nod.

"Alright, Penguin and Bear, go around to the back of the house. Find something to hide behind that still gives you a clear line of sight on the house. Make sure you have at least two clear exits. Go, go."

Bear and Penguin nod. I have to give Bear cred. He's holding up better than I expected. Penguin looks like he's going to start hyperventilating, but he jogs behind Bear. I watch their figures fade into the darkness

"You hold for my mark," I tell Chainy. "No funny stuff. No heroics."

Chainy glares at me. "A Girl Scout could do this."

It was probably a mistake giving him this assignment, but I'm not sure Bear would be fast enough, and I wouldn't trust Penguin to care for a cactus, much less instigate our attack. Chainy and I walk up the driveway together. The cobbles are slick with ice, and I have to focus on each step. My achy hip reminds me of the fall I took at the ice skating rank with Mandy. I glance sideways at Chainy. He looks straight ahead, practically humming with energy. His right eye has turned into a nice shiner over the last few hours.

"You should be more afraid," I tell him.

He is quiet for a moment. "Is Tarren afraid?"

The question catches me off guard, not only for the randomness of injecting Tarren into the conversation, but because Chainy's voice is suddenly soft. Almost...reverent. Weird.

"Tarren's an even bigger idiot than I am," I huff.

Chainy smiles. We both fall into silence. As we crest the driveway, I look at the huge house sitting proudly in front of us. Lotta space for a lotta angels. Four cars sit in the circular driveway – a sexy little Beamer, a black Exodus SUV, a Chevy Tahoe, and a hideous Cadillac that looks like it accidentally showed up to the wrong party.

I spot a bushy fir tree on the left side of the yard. Perfect cover. I get Chainy's attention and point to the tree. He understands. I tell my legs to run, and miraculously, I find myself jogging toward the tree. As soon as I make it, I duck behind its prickly branches, sinking to my knees and wheezing like an asthmatic who also got stung by 100 bees.

The world gets a little bendy, but I wait it out until it's all mostly settled. Back in my glory days, I could have had my new baby locked, loaded, and aimed for damage in forty seconds flat. Now, the minutes tick by as my numb fingers set the tripod. My hands are shaking like a diabetic in need of an insulin shot, and it takes three tries before I get the scope lined up so I can screw it in. I cut out my flashlight as the sky turns purple with dawn above me.

Five minutes, and I'm on my belly in the snow ready to party. The muzzle of the rifle peeks out of the furry branches of the tree, the crosshairs of the scope centered on the front door of the house.

I wave. Chain stands from his crouch behind the SUV and walks up the driveway. My heart starts pounding. I realize again how stupid this is. Hell, my team is so incompetent that they let me come up with the plan. Me!

Chain walks all the way up to the front door. *Go, go, go,* I think, but he lingers a second. He and I debated this during the planning meeting. He wanted to knock or ring the bell, but I know angels. They have some sort of sense about humans. We've seen it out in the field a dozen times, and Maya always seems to know exactly where Tarren and I are in the house. I've never once managed to sneak up on her.

"Go," I hiss under my breath. Chain rushes off the front porch and around the back of the house to meet up with Bear and Penguin.

The front door swings wide. A long-haired teenage boy in a wife beater and jeans leans out. For about half a second, I think we've got the wrong house. We almost never see angels so young, but it has happened. Redmond, Washington is a prime example. I gaze at his face through my binoculars. That sharp look of hunger is so familiar – so angel. He glances both ways.

Just to be sure, I zoom in on his right hand. *Bingo, Yahtzee and Connect Four*. The thick, telltale creases X through his palm. I've seen too many times how the skin peels back and the gross, glowing bulb lifts up ready to feed. It's like something out of a bad Star Trek episode…okay a worse Star Trek episode.

I drop the binoculars and get behind the scope.

Then I send up a tiny prayer to God. *Let my aim be true.* I don't ask for much from him, and my family's sure as hell given up enough. So just this one little favor. I'm thinking about those cans swinging on the branches of the trees in the back yard; the cans I missed again and again. If I fail, we're all dead.

I aim. Breath. Pull.

POW!

The angel crumples just as he turns to pull the door closed.

That's the signal for the Gabettes.

POW, POW, POW! The gunshots come all at once from the back of the house. POW, POW, POW! The sound, so big and deep, spreads out across the wide open sky.

A short girl with long curly hair rushes to the front door and stumbles over the dead angel. She screams, a deep scratchy wail. I switch to the binoculars again, check her palms, and fire another shot as she steps over the body in the doorway.

POW!

The bullet knocks her head back, sending an arc of blood through the air. By the time she collapses three others are crowding through the door.

No thought. No fear. My body knows what to do. My brain makes the calculations. One by one I check their palms, let the binoculars drop around my neck, line up the shot, and take it.

POW! POW! POW!

Bodies fall, but more angels scramble across the lawn. Two are climbing out of windows on the second story, dropping and running.

They're like cockroaches. The largest group of angels Tarren and I have ever come across were the six in Poughkeepsie. I've already put down seven bodies in the last three minutes, and three have slipped by me, rushing down the driveway and into the misty morning.

I'm cussing, shooting, praying. This time I pray for my team, that the shots at the back of the house push the angels toward the front door where I can pick them off.

POW! POW! POW! The gunfire from the back is steady. I take down two more wings as they race across the yard. Then another climbing out of a side window. She tumbles down the roof, leaving a dark, bright stain behind her. Others run past, a lanky teen with a mop of red hair, a short girl with smoke curling from her hands. Somewhere in the back of my brain I wonder at how young they are, at the fear and panic etched on their faces. These aren't the experienced killers we usually fight. These are just kids. And I'm shooting them.

I turn off this part of my brain. *Not grammys or children. Just evil dudes.* We can't feel for them. Mom was adamant about that, and with good reason. You start seeing little bits of humanity in an angel, and then you're going to get so screwed in the head that you won't know up from down.

I push my emotions down. This is a videogame. These are zombies or cyber men or the Borg. I pull the trigger again and again. I don't always get a clean shot. A couple of times my targets stagger, clutching at an arm or a leg as they drag red streaks across the snow. Cries and curses fight the sound of gunfire. One girl begins glowing red, until my bullet douses her light.

POW! POW! POW! Sweat runs into my eyes. How can I be sweating? How long have we been out here? Five minutes? An hour? Ten hours? The gunshots around back are more sporadic. One angel on the rooftop, a chubby girl in bright yellow pajama bottoms, sees the massacre on the front lawn and runs back in the house. I gasp for breath, trying to hold the scope steady as I wait for another figure to dash out the front door or slip from a window.

The scene becomes eerily still.

Where is Maya? Is she in the house? Are they holding her in a cage in the basement? Did she already escape and somehow track down Tarren? Something catches my attention, a thickening pillar of smoke curling up into the sky. It's coming from somewhere behind the house.

A shadow falls across me. I look up, expecting to see an angel standing over me ready to tear my head off, but the shadows come from above. Thick clouds move to cover the pale light of dawn. The wind begins to swirl as if Superman had just let out a sneeze. I clamp a hand on my lucky hat to keep it in place while snow flurries rush into my eyes.

What...the...hell?

Sharp pricks of pain rain across my body. When I crack my eyes open, I see hail plummeting from the sky where snowflakes fell just seconds earlier. A flash rips open the clouds – the biggest pulse of lightening I've ever seen, followed by thunder so loud it feels like we're inside the roar of a lion. The ground rumbles with its aftershock.

I look up, and I see a woman in the sky.

Shit on a stick.

Only certain angels can fly – the ones who call themselves The Exalted.

The most rare and powerful type of angel.

A sphere of lightening slashes down from the sky, and a tree on the other side of the property practically explodes with its impact. Thunder shatters the sky again.

Dear God, this woman could easily kill us all. Somehow, my hands know what to do. They disengage the rifle from the tripod. I press the stock firmly against my shoulder. I don't even give my legs a command, but they stand up. I step out from the tree, exposing my position. I'm only going to get one shot.

*Impossible,* I think as I squint through the scope and tilt the gun up. *I couldn't even hit a can ten yards away, and I'm going to take a woman out of the sky?*

The hail beats against my upturned face and hands and pings off the rifle. The woman's golden hair whips like a halo around her head. I put her in my crosshairs and fight the screaming wind to keep her there. Her attention is turned away toward the pitiful sounding shots still coming from behind the house. She's going to fry my team in a second.

I take a breath. It all goes away, the wind, the noise, the growing fear that the black smoke might have something to do with Maya. In the silence, I lay my finger across the trigger. I killed my first angel when I was thirteen. I thought that shot was impossible too.

I exhale and pull the trigger.

***

# Author End Note

At this point, Gabe's story syncs with Maya's narrative in RISING. If you want to complete the story, flip to Chapter 23 of RISING or start from the beginning to see what Maya and Tarren were up to this whole time. I have to be honest – I went back and forth on whether to keep this ending as I originally wrote it. I love it and many of my beta readers loved it too; however, several beta readers thought this ending was too abrupt and didn't provide closure. I usually hate when stories do that, but in this case it felt right. Gabe is on a precipice. Not only is the mission literally resting on his shoulders, but this is his moment to break through the depressing last two months and move into a future of healing. This is also the final moment before he reunites with his family, a scene told from his, Tarren's, and Penguin's (Rain's) perspectives in Chapter 24 of RISING. Since this book was meant to be read either after or in concert with RISING, I hope you'll forgive me for any frustration this ending might cause. Just remember, this may be the end of Gabe's narrative, but it is not the ending of the full story, which you can find in RISING.

I hope you enjoyed Gabe's unique take on the world. If you loved RECOVERING as much as I enjoyed writing it, please consider leaving a short review. Reviews make a huge difference to indie authors and help us get the word out about our books. Even just a few sentences about your thoughts are very much appreciated!

If you can't get enough of Gabe, Maya, Tarren, and Penguin (aka Bird Brain, Beanpole, and Rain Baily), then it's time to take the leap (sorry, I'm incorrigible) and pick up a copy of LEAPING, Book Four in the series. It'll be a grand old adventure. There's a cowboy. Somebody falls out of a tree (not going to tell you who), and My Little Ponies make a special guest appearance (seriously). How can you say no to that?

***

**Keep In Touch**

Wait, don't go! You just got here. Please come by and say hello if you have time. My website includes a few special extras for my extra special fans (you are extra special, aren't you?). Find me at:

**Mailing List Signup**-- www.JBennettWrites.com/Mailing-List/
Website: www.JBennettWrites.com
Social Media: www.facebook.com/jbennettwrites
Email: JBennett@JBennettWrites.com

# Works by J Bennett :

## *Girl With Broken Wings Series*
Falling *(Book One)*
Coping *(Novella, 1.5)*
Landing *(Book Two)*
Rising *(Book Three)*
Recovering (*Novella, 3.5)*
Leaping *(Book Four) <<< SAMPLE BELOW*
Flying (*Book Five)*

## *The Vampire's Housekeeper Chronicles*
Employment Interview With A Vampire *(Novella #1)*
When Vampires And Ninjas Collide *(Novella #2)*
Apprenticeship With A Vampire *(Novella #3)*
Thanksgiving With The Werewolves (*Novella #4)*

**About J Bennett**

J Bennett lives and writes in San Diego. Her writing partner is a bunny named Avalon who contributes to each manuscript by trying to eat it. His adorableness is his primary strength as a writer.

J Bennett is a professional copywriter and an author who loves asking that oh-so-dangerous question – "What if?" She currently writes a paranormal adventure series, *Girl With Broken Wings,* and a tongue-in-cheek vampire humor short story series, *The Vampire's Housekeeper Chronicles.*

Contact J Bennett at JBennett@JBennettWrites.com.

**Next in the Girl With Broken Wings series:**

# Leaping

## Chapter 2

After we make it through the seizure-inducing laser lights, rolling fog, and gruesome rubber zombies of the "haunted house" on Tucker Cartwright's front lawn, Gabe shouts three names to the beefy thug with a crooked nose who guards the front door. He swipes a big thumb down his iPad and checks us off.

As we push through ornate glass double doors, Gabe turns back and gives us both a proud grin. Beneath his Batman mask, his brown eyes shine with mischief. I wonder if he somehow managed to snag invites for us in less than 24 hours or merely hacked the guest list. His hacker skills are damn impressive, and his keyboard has opened just as many doors for us as his lock pick kit.

I pull in a big breath as we enter into a wide foyer lit by a huge overhead chandelier. A huge mass of humanity slithers against itself. Voices beat against my sensitive ear drums, and the smell of roasted meat assaults my nose.

The auras. They create a second light show that only I can see. They are a great cloud of color throbbing with energy. Calling to me. My hands begin to kindle with heat, and I feel the drowsy monster inside of me stir.

A year ago this entire scene would have fritzed out my brain and sent me tumbling into the abyss of hunger. My body would have trembled like a box of matchsticks inside a washing machine, and the monster would have roared so loud inside of me. I would have lost control.

I push away all those poison thoughts. We'd pulled into a nothing desert town this afternoon, and while Tarren changed the oil in the jeep, I'd set up the Prism and let it flood my body with energy, filling up the vast hole of my hunger. My monster is swollen and full, just a minor demon I must keep my eye on. I clench my jaw, steel my spine.

Tarren's eyes are on my face, and I know he's searching for weakness. He reaches up and unmutes his earpiece. "We split up and canvas," he says as a drunk Cleopatra stumbles past, her ankles wobbling in golden, strappy stilettos.

At a nearby bar, an aging Tinker Bell with a smooth, frozen face sips a drink and gives Tarren an appreciative oggle.

"Check," I confirm.

"Check," Gabe says, his head swiveling. "Whoa, yeah, that lady looks really suspicious over there." His gaze is trained on a gorgeous woman almost popping out of her Princess Lea costume as she leans against the bar. "Yep, I'm definitely going to have to give her a very thorough visual and physical assessment," he says and plows into the crowd.

"If you lay eyes on him do not engage," Tarren says. "We'll

regroup and find a way to isolate and strike." His eyes are a pale blue, the same color as mine. I used to think those eyes were an endless winter tundra, but now I know the wellspring of emotion they hide so well. What is it that I see in his gaze now as he meets mine? Is it respect, acceptance, or am I looking too hard, trying to see what I want to see?

"I'll take the left wing of the house. Gabe, you're at the front. Maya, right wing and patio." With his orders given, Tarren turns away, his coat whirling with him. I watch his hat bob in the crowd before disappearing into the mass of bodies. Both of my brothers possess a handheld thermal night vision imager, which can usually help them pinpoint the low body heat that an angel registers, but I wonder how useful the heat sensing cameras will be in this crowded party scene. Luckily, my own eyes serve as my primary angel-hunting tool. I start toward my assigned area, noting immediately that the crowds are thinner in this part of the home. Tarren must have seen this too. I let my gaze roam around a sparely populated lounge and then a more crowded man cave where a cluster of men lounge around a huge television, game controllers in hand. Each partygoer possesses a shining aural glow around them. All human.

As soon as my enhanced eyes land on a person without an aura, I'll have my angel.

I make a quick circuit of a room filled with signed guitars mounted on the wall. Two women make out with impressive gusto, their hands groping without shame and pretense. I pause momentarily, watching their auras flush with deep, wine-colored purples. Lust. Their auras rage with it, dancing along their bodies like they were both aflame with color.

I duck out of the room and take a deep breath.

"Hello."

I spin away from the arm attempting to drape over me.

"Whoa, whoa, skittish, huh?"

I turn and look into the rock hard pecs of a guy dressed as a Spartan who might have literally wandered off the set of *300*.

"Nice panties," I huff, trying to shake off the feel of his aura. Mr. Muscles is very human, very handsome, and very drunk. I can tell by the way his blue-green aura sloshes within his aura.

"Thanks," he grins at me. "Like my cape?" He holds it out, nearly knocking the tiara off a skanky Cinderella. "Hello," he slurs to her as I slip away. I move back toward the center of the house. Gabe chats up Princess Lea at the bar. When she throws her head back in a pretty laugh, his eyes quickly scan the hands of everyone else at the bar. He won't find any telltale slits in palms. I see auras all around.

"There you are Nursey." My Spartan is back at my side in all his beefy glory.

Gabe spots me and gives me a big thumbs up.

"You come with anyone?" the Spartan asks. His boots squeak against the tiles as I move toward the patio doors. "I'm not asking for myself. My roommate just broke up with his girlfriend, and I'ma just trying to fix 'em up."

"That's really nice of you," I say as I squeeze past a couple dressed as Woody and Buzz Lightyear.

"Yeah, I'm a great guy," Spartan says. "My friend is too. His name is Philip. He does accounting or somethin' for like, lots of movie studios. Drives a Beamer."

A gorgeous woman in a toga holds out a tray of

appetizers. "Salmon spinach cakes?" she offers.

"Uh, no thanks," I murmur.

"Don't mind if I do," Mr. Muscles says, reaching over me to grab two appetizers off the tray. The whiff of fish tightens my stomach, and I have to make an effort to remind myself that I would have once shoveled those little spinach cakes into my mouth like a conveyor belt. Back when I was fully human. Normal

"You an actress?" my Spartan asks as he pops both appetizers into his mouth. "I'm an actor. Ever hear of the BoFlexion 4,000? I was a fitness model for the infomercial."

"Wow, so cool." I push open the finely etched glass door to the patio. A gust of temperate air greets me was I walk onto the lavish outdoor space. Clumps of people huddle around tables or lean against a balcony.

"Yeah, yeah, watch this." Mr. Spartan sucks in a deep breath and says, "Just use the BoFlexion 4,000 for ten minutes a day, and the fat will melt off your body." As he speaks, the man slowly lifts his arms up and down and twists side to side, a serious expression plastered across his face. "See, that's what I did, for the uh…uh…"

"Infomercial?"

"Hey, is that a gun?"

His eyes are on my holster, and I quickly put a hand down to cover it. "I'm a nurse during the zombie apocalypse." I walk over to the balcony and turn, leaning my back against the railing. This position allows me to gaze through the large glass windows back into the house. This is a good vantage point. I watch bodies move by, painted faces, wild hair, shining costumes, bright auras.

"Oh yeah, I get that." Beefcakes chuckles as he leans against the balcony next to me. "So, are you interested in, like, hooking up with my friend, cause otherwise I gotta find another girl. I have a boyfriend by the way, so I'm taken."

"Aw shucks," I say. He grins, and damn, he is so hot I think I could fry an egg on his hairless, rock hard abs. "Actually, I...I kind of have a boyfriend, too." Why are my words suddenly soft and hesitant? Rain's face comes front and center in my brain, bringing back floods of worry with it.

"But hey, look." I point to a Miley Cyrus lookalike huddled on a bench a few feet away. Her thin shoulders shake, and the mascara roading down her cheeks would tell me she isn't having a good night even if I couldn't see the rippling oranges of humiliation. "She looks like she might need a picker-upper."

Beefcakes follows my gaze and then looks back at me with a grin. "Nice meetin' you Nursey."

"Your roommate is lucky."

"Definitely." He grabs up his drink and starts toward weepy Miley on slightly unsteady steps.

I unmute my earpiece. "Nothing in the right wing or on the patio."

Clanging pots and hisses suddenly sound. "Left wing is clean," Tarren says. "Checking the kitchen now"

"Don't see him...on the...dance floor," Gabe hollers over the blare of music.

I look up at the row of lighted windows above. "Second floor," Tarren and I say at the same time. Damn, that little jinx show has been happening more and more often.

I give my Spartan a quick wave as I stroll back into the zoo of people. After a little exploration, I find a massive spiral staircase guarded by two hulking goons. Apparently hulking goons are a real thing in Beverly Hills. Just to make the point, a stupid red velvet rope hangs between two poles set in front of the lowest stair. I pull out my phone, pretending to text as I lean against a pillar and watch them. Tarren and then Gabe join me a minute later. I'm not even asking about all the glitter on Gabe's costume.

In three minutes of observation, we watch the two trolls turn away a frantic Cher lookalike who begs for a bathroom as well as a highly blitzed cheerleader who doesn't seem to realize that she's not at her own house. They lift the red velvet rope for a refined vampire who escorts a young, giggling pirate girl up with him.

"Angel," I say, watching the girl's bright aura dance against the nothingness coming from the man's trim body.

"Vampire?" Tarren asks.

I nod.

"That wasn't Cartwright," Gabe says.

The three of us ponder.

Tarren's expression is hard. "Too many unknowns. Too many risks."

Classic Tarren move – when the situation changes, pull out and re-assess.

But Gabe doesn't play by those rules, not when innocent lives are on the line. On cue, he shakes his head. "No time. Angel-vamp is going to suck that girl dry if we don't stop him. Who knows how many other wings we've got up there? They could all be using this party as their own personal buffet."

The decision was made the moment an innocent life was at stake. If Tarren was at this party alone, I have no doubt he's already be leaping over the velvet rope, storming the stairs with guns blazing. But he's got us to think about, and Tarren will always hesitate, always tarry to keep us safe. We are his Achilles Heel, which is why I have to convince my brother of what he already knows.

"We've got to go now, Tarren," I say. "Or those lives are on us."

Our eyes meet. He's too good at controlling his aura, keeping it tight around his tall frame without any flickers of emotion. "We need to be careful," is all he says to betray his unease.

"Step one: distract the guards, get them out of the way," Gabe says. "I can tell them a fight's breaking out on the dance floor."

"They'll call it in," Tarren responds. He nods to the center room. "Four roaming security personnel."

"Okay, got another plan," Gabe responds.

"I've got a better one," I tell him.

Gabe scoffs. "My plans are the best. Four out of five crime fighters prefer Gabe's plans over the leading competition."

"You," I stare at him, "bring the jeep up. We'll probably need a quick exit." I look at Tarren, "You come with me. Act drunk."

Gabe gives me a sour face. "Batman doesn't drive the getaway car."

I ignore him and pull my top lower as I stumble out from behind the pillar and let out a high, squealing laugh. Tarren walks beside me and tries to smile. "Let me do all the talking," I murmur, because, let's be honest, a piece of plywood could give Tarren a run for his money when it comes to acting. My brothers were homeschooled by our mother, Diana, between her angel-killing missions, but if they'd gone to real school, I have no doubt that sulky miniature Tarren would have been assigned "tree", "bush", or "guy on bus reading paper," in every school play.

"Hey there, helllooo!" I call to the goons and hiccup. "Are you guys, dressed like...like...CIA agents, or something? Cause it looks really good. Really good!"

Troll Number One's mouth twitches up in a smile he quickly squelches.

"Sorry Miss, you're not allowed up here."

"No, no, no." I lean in close to Troll Number One as if whispering a secret. "Some vampire guy, he told us to go upstairs. That ah, Tucker, Tucker Cartwright, he like...wants to see me and him." I jerk my head toward Tarren. "We're a, uh...brother and sister act, if you know what I mean...at least we are for Tucker Cartwright." I laugh again.

Troll Number Two brings his phone up.

"Noooooooo." I place my hand on his arm. "It's a surprise for Tucker. We're a present. Right?" I hiccup and look at Tarren.

"Yes, a surprise," Tarren says softly.

"And what about him?" Troll Number One points a beefy finger behind us. I don't even have to turn around. The feel of Gabe's aura is as distinct as every other part of him. "Mr. Cartwright has a type."

"That vampire dude paid me $500. Said Mr. Cartwright likes it when people watch and he has a..." Gabe lowers his voice and tilts between us, "a certain childhood Batman fetish. It's $500, so I'm not arguing. Whatever he wants. I can watch. I can join in the fun. I can piss on his face. You know, meet all his needs. Batman lives to serve the citizens of Gotham." He cracks a rueful smile.

"The guy said we're not supposed to keep Tucker waiting," I say, putting on a worried voice.

"Let 'em through," Troll Number One says.

I give him a big, sloppy grin as he unhooks the stupid velvet rope and allows us access to the staircase. "You guys are the best. Oh My God, Tucker Cartwright. This is unbelievable," I gush as we head up the stairs. As soon as the goons are behind us, I give Gabe an angry glare.

"Piss on his face?"

"Batman doesn't drive the getaway car," Gabe says again as we reach the second floor and survey a long hallway filled with closed doors.

"They'll be able to give descriptions of us to law enforcement," Tarren says. I'm probably imaging the icicles of unhappiness dripping off his words.

"Gabe's got his mask, you've got your cowboy hat, and I'm wearing a wig. It's fine," I hiss back at him.

Tarren decides to generously withhold any additional rebukes. "How many humans up here?" he asks.

I lower a barrier in my mind, let the angel part of me extend. Heat roils through my hands, and the seams in my palms pull, asking for release. I feel the auras of my brothers so close and the mass of energy throbbing downstairs. I push, focusing my mind on this hallway.

"Multiple humans up here. There and there," I point to two rooms in the hallway. Their auras lick against that sensitive part of my brain. "We have to be careful."

"Don't see any cameras," Gabe says, scanning up and

down the hallway. "Small favors."

Tarren is quiet for a moment, just a moment, as his mind calculates. We could be facing two angels up here or a dozen behind every door. And we've got humans in the mix.

Tarren's lips press tight. The plan is woven. "We go room by room," he says. "Use the heat sensor to identify and then clip all the wings we find. Tranq any humans. Do it quick. Do it clean. No alarms. I'll take the first three doors. Gabe the next three. Maya, those two on the other side."

"I didn't bring a tranq gun," I admit, "but I don't sense any humans in my rooms."

Tarren gives me a look that says, *We'll discuss this later.*

*You try finding a place for two guns and a phone while wearing ten square inches of clothing,* I think back at him.

"Exit point?" Gabe's voice is low, finally serious. I watch the teasing greens drain from his aura, leaving it a dark blue, the color of the ocean on a cloudy, unhappy day.

"There." Tarren points to one of the doors. "According to the layout, that should be the bathroom. There'll be a window that lets out on the side of the house. As soon as your rooms are cleared, get the bodies out and straight back to the car."

"Should have bought my bat grappling hook," Gabe grumbles.

Tarren's eyes are gray and hard as flint. I study his smooth, controlled aura. *Does he still get nervous?* I wonder. Especially with a job like this. So many ways this could melt down. All it would take is a single human letting out a scream, or an angel with a power we've never seen before. I pull in a deep, long breath and nod my assent.

"Right on," Gabe says.

"Quick, quiet, clean," Tarren says. Our new team motto.

We each turn away, moving toward our assigned doors. Adrenaline sloshes through my veins, and I've grown used to this sick anticipation. Blood and bullets. *Unless it's one of us tonight,* I think. That familiar knot of dread is back, sitting heavily in my stomach. I know that we cannot jump through the fire forever without getting burned ourselves.

My heels softly plow the thick carpet as I wrap my gloved hand around the first door. My right hand is already cradling my Glock in a strong grip. No human auras within the room, but that doesn't mean an angel isn't waiting to jump out at me like the rubber zombies in the haunted tunnel. I turn the door handle, and the door opens into an office. My gun is up, ready, sweeping the parameter. My eyes search the shadows and find nothing.

I close the door softly behind me. My prickling angel sense feels the auras of my brothers up here with me. A muffled shot rings from one of the other rooms, seemingly so loud, but I know the pounding music downstairs will drown it out. I wish the silencers they show in the movies really existed. They don't. Silencers muffle a shot, but it's still loud. Still a risk.

I move to the second door. The knob resists my hand. *Locked.*

On any other mission I'd have a lock pick kit squirreled away in an inner pocket, but in this tight, nothing-there costume, I come up empty. I'm so not asking my brothers for an assist. I turn the knob harder. My muscles tense. I imagine all my hybrid angel strength pouring out of me into the knob. *Come on, dammit. What's the point of having super strength if I can't...* something snaps within the handle and it turns willingly in my grasp.

I shake out my throbbing hands. Point to hybrid angel girl!

I open the door slowly and move into a vast room. *Damn...* I've never been across the ocean, but I'm pretty sure a European castle could fit into this room.

*Whoa, narcissistic much?* My eyes travel around the room. Tucker Cartwright, Tucker Cartwright, Tucker Cartwright. He gives me that swarmy grin from the beach, from behind the wheel of an old Corvette, leaning up against a lamp post in the rain with the Eiffel Tower behind him. Not phallic at all. His posters and calendars and portraits compete with each other to fill up every possible inch of space on the walls. Was this room decorated by a 12-year-old girl? I'm surprised I don't see magazine cutouts encircled by huge hearts taped to the walls.

I catch a figure looming in my peripheral and spin, almost blowing the head right off a life-sized cardboard cutout of Tucker Cartwright. The cutout grins at me, his eyes saying, *Yeah I'm hot. Wanna fuck?*

"Shit!" a voice hollers from a massive bed sitting in the middle of the room.

I turn and shoot, but the man is already rolling out of the bed. My first bullet kicks a hole through his pillow. He hits the floor with a thud, all bare ass and skinny legs. Tucker Cartwright. *So not pleased to meet you.* I aim for his chest, but he puts a hand up, and I'm off my feet flying through the air.

I take out the cardboard cutout before I hit the wall hard and slide to the ground. *Telekinesis, dammit!* The room is all floaty, a thousand Tucker Cartwrights sloshing up and down the walls. I shake away the dizziness as I jump to my feet.... and notice the gun is nowhere near my grip.

"You wicked cunt!" Tucker Cartwright hisses, and I hear the door slam behind me. "You're one of 'em whatchamacallem? The...the Vigils?"

He folds his arms around his chest like he is madly, truly offended. "And crashing my fucking party. Probably ate a fuck ton of my shrimp too, didn't you?" I find my gun firmly couched beneath the sole of his foot. "God, I can't believe this." He looks at me and runs a hand through his long, tousled hair. "What the hell is wrong with your aura?"

Bad. This is very bad. I always knew this vigilante life would put me in a coffin at an early age, but seriously, Tucker Cartwright? The world's lamest fake famous person whose vocabulary consists 50% of the word Fuck?

"Oh wait. Wait. Wait. Wait!" Tucker says as he leans over and picks up my gun. "You're that girl, the half angel." His eyes are wide, and his mouth turns up into a cruel smile. "War said that you were dead. Burned to a crisp."

"War." The word is growl out of my throat as Warren's ugly face flashes across my memory. I haven't gotten around to killing that grotesque sack of shit yet, but he's high up on the priority list.

Tucker hefts my gun. He moves a step closer, and I hold my ground. My muscles are tense. If I were facing a human I wouldn't be nervous at all. Slow, fat-fingered humans. But another angel – a full-fledged angel is another ballgame. Tucker is faster than me, stronger too. All of my enhanced abilities are shadows compared to what a full angel can do.

*Stall,* I think. *Distract him. Get out of his shooting path.* "How's my buddy War doing?" I ask and give Tucker a flashy smile of my own.

"He's doing well, pushing the angel religion shit," Tucker says as he takes a step forward. "They lap it up."

Behind Tucker's naked ass, I noticed a figure sprawled in the bed on top of the cheetah coverlet. The long-legged woman is naked and dead, and her thick black hair fans out across the black satin sheets. Tucker's body glows with the ethereal energy he soaked up from the woman.

Tucker must notice my gaze. He gives me a smile that almost drips with slime. "It's ridiculously easy. They're so excited, so innocent." He nods toward the bed and pitches his voice into a high falsetto. "Ooohhh Tucker Cartwright, I'll suck your dick if you give my headshot to your agent."

The asshole laughs. Actually laughs. And that's when I decide that Tucker Cartwright definitely won't be killing me tonight.

"And their eyes," Tucker says. "They get so big and scared as I drain the life out of them." He looks at the bed again. "That one hardly fought at all."

He's brimming with the power of his recent feed. It's making him cocky and stupid. I can work with that.

"How do you get away with it?"

"Heroine overdose. So tragic," he says and tilts his head. I see the spoon and syringe on the nightstand. "All these young actresses. Hollywood just chews them up and spits them out."

I move, dashing right. BOOM! The gun goes off. Then I'm on top of Tucker. My blade flashes in my hand. I see the slap of surprise on features as my dagger puts a red smile across his neck, from ear to ear. His telekinesis explodes, throwing me hard into the ceiling. The plaster cracks and rains down as I fall. I tuck my body. The landing isn't graceful, but I roll and keep all my bones intact as I make it to my feet. In a distant place, my elbow throbs with muted pain.

The gunshot. I look down as panic spreads like ice in my chest. Was I hit? Specks of blood dot my chest like tiny rubies, but I don't see a big gaping hole. No rivulets of blood run down my arms or legs or spread a wet puddle across my costume. The flecks of blood aren't mine.

Near the foot of the bed, Tucker spills his blood across the white travertine tiles. I watch the liquid pump from his wound and slide across the floor in a crimson wave. My stomach tightens, and the normal college sophomore I used to be screams somewhere far, far in the back of my mind.

Tucker grabs his neck as if he could hold his severed artery together. As if he could save the life I've already taken from him. I stand in front of him, watching, waiting, trying to remember that he is a very bad person and deserves to die.

The gunshot was muted by the silencer, but it was still loud. It could bring Troll One and Two rushing up the stairs. I know this, but my legs don't move. I have to watch. No matter how bad Tucker Cartwright was, I must stand vigil for his last moments. My eyes keep flicking away from the shuddering body, but everywhere they go, they see Tucker again and again and again like his ghost is accusing me from every poster.

Tucker's hand hits the tile with a wet thud. His face is ghastly pale, mouth open, eyes half-lidded. The glow is gone from his ashen skin. A few more tiny bubbles of blood slip down from the corner of his mouth, and then Tucker Cartwright's life is over. But his face, all his thousand faces will be safe inside my perfect memory forever.

My legs are shaky as I force them to move toward the bed.

"I'm sorry," I whisper to the young woman who stares at me with unseeing brown eyes. She truly is beautiful. I bet she was one of those people who everyone described as "full of life." Not anymore. I carefully lift her body with one arm and pull the big cheetah print comforter off the bed before setting her back down. I don't have time for this, but I pull the black silk sheet over her body, covering her nakedness. It's pointless. The police will bag and tag her. She'll be naked on a slab in a morgue in a few hours, but right now in this quiet moment when her parents and siblings and all her friends still believe she is alive, she deserves to be covered.

I toss the comforter on the floor, keeping it away from the spreading crimson puddle of Tucker's blood. The liquid catches in the grout between the tiles and runs down them like a frisky stream.

Trying not to look at his face or the gaping wound I put into his neck, I lift Tucker's limp body and drop him onto the comforter. Blood still dribbles from his wound.

*Shit, I killed Tucker Cartwright.* The thought is almost absurd, but here I am, rolling his body into a cheetah print log.

*Gun.*

I turn and find my gun sitting in the puddle of Tucker's blood. My blonde wig lies nearby, looking like a mangled Pomeranian. I'm starting to shake now, and time seems to be pulsing in my veins instead of blood. Did Tucker scream? Are the goons coming?

I shove the wig on my head, twisting it the right way and shoving escaped wisps of my hair inside. Then I reach into the blood and grab the glistening gun and push it awkwardly into my holster. I feel wetness sliding down my leg. The throbbing in my elbow intensifies. I look up at the ceiling, at the long crack my body made when Tucker launched me upwards.

*That's definitely going to be a mind fuck for the police.*

I look around the room again, at the pillow with the charred bullet hole in its center, at the pale starlet wannabe shrouded in the black sheets, and finally at the pool of Tucker's blood. It seems darker now, more wet. Should I try to clean up? Did I leave DNA on the ceiling?

*Get out. Just get out. Think through the rest later.*

I grunt and sling Tucker's bundled body over my shoulder. His bare feet dangle as I walk across the room and cautiously open the door. Just as I step out, a door across the hall flings open. The female pirate, her costume shoved down to her hips, stumbles out. She sobs loudly, way too loudly, and mascara-tinted tears lance down her cheeks.

I quickly set down my cargo and hold up my blood-stained hands.

"Hey, hey, hey." I open my arms and she tumbles into them. Her body shudders violently, all that delicious energy heaving against me. Her energy is music to me. *Sweet music.* I can hear it inside the inner cavities of my mind, plucking beautiful harp strings. Another time, another place, I wouldn't have been strong enough to resist all that energy, all that fear.

"Help. I....need...he's dead....he killed him....Batman....we have to call the...the...."

"Shhhhhh," I say to her gently as my fingers find the carotid artery in her neck. I press firmly.

"Stop. Wait.....wait..." the girl mumbles. She tries to break out of my embrace, but her efforts are nothing compared to my strength. I keep my hold, and watch the red spikes of fear fade as her aura flattens. When her legs give out, I catch her.

"You missed one," I say to Gabe who stands in the doorway panting hard.

"He had three girls in there with 'em," Gabe says. "I got Red Riding Hood and the witch. Man, Red Riding Hood gave me quite a chase. You good on your end?"

"Tucker Cartwright." I nod toward the bundle at my feet. I carry the limp pirate back into the room. "Got a little bloody."

Gabe's angel – the vampire – is sprawled on a huge, luxurious bed, now sporting a perfect round hole in his forehead. The two unconscious girls are laid out nicely on the pillows beside him. The half-dressed witch has a tranq dart in her arm. I don't see a dart in Red Riding Hood.

"Pull the sheet and wrap him up," I tell Gabe.

"Yep." He shoves the vampire off the bed, and the body thuds against the floor. "Any of that blood yours?"

So that's why his voice is so hard.

I lay pirate girl down next to her sleeping companions. "No, it's Tucker's. Had to use my dagger. It got dicey." I realize the bad pun only after I say it.

"I don't like dicey." It's not the way Gabe says it, but the flare of his aura, those spikes of pained reds, that feels like a punch.

He rolls up the vampire in the crisp white sheet, turning him into a life-sized bowling pin. A ruby stain immediately begins to form and metastasize near the top.

"Time to go. Tarren's probably waiting for us."

Gabe grunts, and wobbling only a little, heaves the swathed vampire over his shoulder. When we make it back to the hallway, I reload Tucker onto my shoulder. Thank god the two trolls didn't come upstairs and find his bundled corpse laying in the middle of the hallway.

"There," Gabe points to a door that opens up into a Jack and Jill bathroom. I twist the crystal knob, and damn, the bathroom is so big you could probably fit an entire cheerleading squad inside and still have room for the basketball team in the stone shower to the side.

"God, why are so many bad guys so rich?" Gabe says behind me.

"Batman is rich too," I point out. Already, the shaking is beginning to quiet in my limbs. That endless crimson puddle of Tucker's blood is retreating from my mind as my training kicks in.

I spot a long, thin window that sits about six feet up from the tub. I reach up, slide it open, and punch out the screen.

"You go first, bring the car around," I say.

"Batman doesn't…" Gabe starts.

"…unless you want to shove these guys through that window."

Gabe looks at the distance from floor to window. He's strong for his size, but I know he doesn't want to try shoulder pressing two hundred pounds of dead weight over his head. "Lady's choice," he says and gives me a gracious little bow before stepping into the tub.

"You need any help?" I ask Gabe teasingly. "I can give you a boost." The window is small, high up. Most humans wouldn't be able to manage it without a step ladder and a serious diet.

"In case you've forgotten, I was skvyying my skinny ass through tiny windows in giant, rich-guy bathrooms long before you ever joined this club," Gabe says. Then he sticks his tongue out. "Plus, Batman can always handle himself."

He grabs the window ledge and swings his body up and out in one fluid motion.

"Batman has a fucking butler," I remind him.

I hear him laugh, and then his fingertips disappear from the ledge. I listen and hear the faint impact as he hits the ground below and cusses.

I wait, watching the weird blobby shape the blood makes on the white sheet covering the vampire.

"It's clear," Gabe says into my ear piece. "No eyes out here."

And then it's time for my hat trick. I start with Tucker, who is smaller and thinner than his vampire friend. I boost him back onto my shoulder and step into the empty tub. I know that Tucker is dead, but I still tense up, half expecting a hand to come shooting out from the cover to wrap around my neck.

*Get a grip,* I tell myself. With a quick bend of the knees, I press Tucker over my head and shove him through the window. He gets a little stuck, but I push, and then he's gone, tumbling into the night.

The vampire is much more stubborn. His body is unwieldy in the thin sheet, and I almost lose him as I struggle to get him overhead. He's all muscle, tall, and heavy, with broad shoulders and a barrel chest that does not want to go through the window. I get his legs out, but his chest gets stuck. I keep seeing that growing red stain over his head, the locks of dark hair peeking out from the top of the sheet.

*Dammit, go!*

I shove his shoulders, scooting him out little by little. *Dear God, what if we have to cut him up?* I left my bone saw in my other nurse's costume. That joke isn't even funny. I've seen a lot of gruesomeness in the past year, but I'm not sure I could handle hacking off limbs and spilling out intestines. With one final, brutal shove, the vampire clears the window and drops like a stone. I almost feel bad for the police who are going to have to investigate this crazy mess of a crime scene.

In one smooth motion, I grasp the window's edge and slide my body through the narrow opening. I let go of the ledge and drop two stories into the bushes below. My landing is soft, but the impact jars my elbow and the other sore places where I took a beating curtesy of Tucker's telekinesis. I'll see what pretty bruise art I have as soon as we get clear of this place.

I collect my scattered cargo from the bushes. Just as I pull my soggy vampire from a flattened bush, the jeep pulls up, headlights off. Gabe jumps out and opens the back. We both pick up a body.

"Screen was still in the window," Gabe says to me as if I hadn't noticed that one part of our trio is conspicuously absent. The bodies land heavily in the back, *wump, wump,* one after the other.

"Maybe Tarren took another way out," I say without conviction.

"He never deviates unless there's a problem," Gabe says. He switches his ear piece back on. "Batman, check, nurse check. Wings are clipped. Cargo loaded. What's your status sheriff?"

We wait for Tarren's check-in.

Nothing.

"If he doesn't check in, he'd want us to wait ten minutes and then go," I say with no conviction. Gabe and I look at each other. We are of one mind.

"You climb back up through the window," Gabe says. "I'll get back in through the front and meet you upstairs."

Just as I nod, something hurdles out of the window and lands with a *SMACK* on the ground. *Tarren!* My heart nearly explodes. I stumble forward, staring at the unmoving object.

"Watch out, another one coming," Gabe says, touching my arm. His aura stings, snapping me through the cloud of my fear just as another dark shape plummets to the ground. I look up at the window just as two boots slide out, followed by legs and Tarren's big body. It's amazing he can even squeeze his wide shoulders through that tiny opening. He drops hard and rolls, his hat speeding away from him. When he stands up, Tarren favors an ankle. A single trickle of sweat rolls down his temple.

"Everything okay?" I pick up his hat and hand it to him.

"Are you injured?" Tarren's eyes are planted on the bloody smears on my costume.

"It wasn't pretty, but I got it done." I lean down and pick up one of the sheet-wrapped bodies.

Tarren bends to collect the other body, but Gabe steps up, blocking him. "Next time, check in," he says. His gaze holds Tarren, and all of Gabe's smiles and jokes are buried beneath the red fear that streaks through his aura.

Tarren nods, and I wonder as I so often do how the one could possibly survive if the other were lost. I got a glimpse of that chaotic ruin last year when Gabe almost died...because of what I did...what I became. I push those thoughts away. The mission isn't over yet.

"We need to go," Tarren says, and Gabe moves out of his way. Tarren and I drop the final two bodies into the back of the jeep. His aura hugs low to his body, almost as gray as his eyes.

*Craptastic.* His eyes only shift from blue to gray when he's angry. Is he still mad about the fact that I didn't have a tranq gun, or is this entire mission just giving him the heebie jeebies, like me? He's holding his aura down with all the control he possesses, and I can't read anything off it.

"We need to go," is all he says.

Tarren closes the back door on our silent cargo. I let out my breath, feeling like I was just released from an incredibly tight corset. This mission could have turned into a shit hurricane in a hundred different ways, but we improvised, and we took four very bad people out of commission permanently. I wasn't fast enough to save that poor dead girl lying in Tucker Cartwright's bed, but there are other starlets who will live to audition another day because of me.

We did a good thing. Won another small battle.

I open my mouth to say something profound and encouraging to my weary team when my phone dings with an incoming message.

*Shit.* Rain knows I'm on a mission. He shouldn't text...unless.

Gabe says something behind me, but I don't hear it as my hands tear into my holster, digging out my phone. Stupid fingers. I press too hard, and the slider on the screen doesn't move. I take a little breath, and try again, slower. This time the phone opens. I jab at my passcode and then slap the message icon. My breath turns into a garbled sob as I read the message. *Hurt. Help. Enterprise.*